I was lying on my bed telling my best friend my latest theory about earthquakes. My bedroom walls, which were cluttered with posters of rock stars my junior year, plastered with sports figures my sophomore year, and papered with pink cabbage roses (my mother's choice) when I was a freshman, were, for my senior year, painted a pristine white and absolutely blank. I felt that they mirrored my life, which was also a total blank, along with being boring, boring, boring. . . .

I got up off the bed and went over to my dresser. I thought I felt a slight movement beneath my feet.

I turned to Jennifer. "Did you feel the floor move?"

"You're imagining it," she said. "Sometimes I think you're willing an earthquake to happen."

"Maybe I am," I said. Maybe wanting something to change in my life was enough to do it. Maybe, by concentrating really hard, I could change the world.

"Of course it will be. It'll be totally different. For one thing, we won't be living at home."

Most of the time I didn't feel like I was living at home anyway. Most of the time I felt invisible at home. Sometimes I thought that the earth could open up and swallow me and my parents wouldn't even notice.

"And for another," said Jennifer, "there will be all those new guys."

And I'd still be going with Eddie.

"It won't be all that different," I said again.

"What's with you, anyway? You're really in a strange mood today."

"It's our anniversary," I said.

"You and Eddie?"

I nodded.

"And that's depressing you?"

I sat up in the sand and looked out over the water. I watched the waves breaking with their usual predictability. I kept hoping just one wouldn't break. Just a little one.

"Don't you ever wish something magical would happen?" I asked.

"Are you back on the subject of earthquakes again?"

"What if just once the sun didn't set over the water?" I asked.

Jennifer rolled her eyes.

"What if just once the sky would be green?"

Jennifer sat up and gave me a worried look.

"Why does everything have to be so predictable?" I practically shouted.

"Come on," said Jennifer, "what you need is a good long swim."

What I needed was a change. I just didn't know what it was.

2

WE WERE SITTING IN THE LAST ROW OF THE MOVIE THEATER and Eddie had his arm around me. We weren't holding hands, but I knew we would be as soon as we finished off the popcorn. I knew this because Eddie was predictable just like everything else in my life.

Once in a while he stopped chewing long enough to nuzzle my neck with his lips, which he thought was a move that really turned me on. All it really did was get my neck greasy from the butter and gritty from the salt and make me want to go to the restroom and wash it off, but I wouldn't because I didn't want to hurt Eddie's feelings.

Because it was the second anniversary of our first real date and from certain none-too-subtle hints he had let drop, I knew that he had mistakenly gotten the impression that this was going to be *the night*. I knew the way Eddie thought, and what he was thinking was that taking me to the movie I wanted to see would get me warmed up, otherwise he would never have agreed to go to a tearjerker like the one we were watching. After the movie it was on to the beach party, only this time when the couples paired off and started disappearing behind the rocks with their blankets under their arms, we'd be one of those couples, and this time we wouldn't just be fooling around.

The movie was already totally ruined for me because I hadn't been able to concentrate on it for a minute. We could just as well have gone to some adventure film Eddie would have liked.

He leaned over and did his neck nuzzle for a moment, murmuring, "I love you, Kathy," in my ear at the same time. I pretended to be very interested in the movie while in reality I was wishing that the big earthquake would hit at that exact moment because otherwise I didn't know how I was going to get out of it.

Big earthquake were magic words in California because the countdown was on and the scientists were expecting it any time. Very much like previews of coming attractions in movie theaters, we had been getting lots of jolts in the last couple of years, just in case anyone started to forget that we were due for the big one.

So I was wishing for an earthquake, but at the same time I knew I wasn't going to be that lucky.

And poor Eddie had done nothing to deserve the fact that I found an earthquake preferable to making love with him.

We met on the school playground when we were both eight. I don't remember what we fought about, but I ended up breaking one of Eddie's front teeth. Luckily his father was a dentist so my parents didn't have to pay for it. After that we became best buddies. At ten we cut our thumbs, held them together, and became blood brothers forever. We were best friends all through junior high, but when we started high school, it became apparent to me that girls weren't supposed to have boys as best friends and I became friends with Jennifer. At the same time Eddie was going out for sports and hanging out with the guys. As a result, we drifted apart that year. But during the summer after our first year of high school, you were supposed to have a boyfriend or girlfriend and Eddie and I started going out together. We'd always loved each other, neither of us was attracted to anyone else, and it seemed the natural thing to do.

So even though I called Jennifer my best friend, Eddie was really my best friend, along with being my boyfriend. Which made me wonder what was wrong with me. Why couldn't I just be honest with him and say, *Eddie, I just don't feel like doing it?*

I looked over to where Jennifer was sitting, four rows down and on the aisle. The movie was crowded and we hadn't been able to find seats together. It looked as though Alan was all over her and she wasn't doing much to fight him off.

It was their first date, but Alan had a reputation for coming on heavy on a first date. Normally I didn't think Jennifer would put up with it, but knowing Jennifer, she was probably hoping that: 1) Steve was also in the audience; 2) he had seen her; and 3) he was now dying of jealousy. It was a delusion, of course, but one we all have at one time or another.

My own delusion was that I could keep putting off Eddie indefinitely. Two years is a long time.

Eddie finished the popcorn, put the container on the floor, and slid down in his seat. He was now resting his head on my shoulder. He grabbed my hand, pulled it over and placed it on his thigh. Okay, no big deal. I could live with my hand on his thigh.

"You enjoying this bomb?" Eddie whispered to me.

I gave his thigh a pat, but I didn't speak. I acted as though I were totally involved in the movie.

Eddie, in what I'm sure he thought was a sly move, slid his head down until his chin was resting against my right breast. There was a time a move like that on Eddie's part would have raised my blood pressure a few degrees. Now, however, it didn't seem any more exciting than holding his hand, and I ignored it. I wondered why Eddie didn't turn me on anymore.

I started thinking, *Maybe I should let him tonight. Maybe that's what's missing. Maybe it's all a natural progression that I've prematurely put a stop to and maybe if we did it, I'd get back the feelings I used to have whenever he touched me.* But maybe I wouldn't, and that's what scared me. Because there really wouldn't be anything to look forward to.

Eddie and I had to be the only couple I knew who weren't sleeping together. When we first started going out, I just assumed that we would get around to it sooner or later. Here we were at the "later" and the whole situation still confused me.

After two years of going out, even *I* didn't buy my excuses anymore. Compared to how other guys might have acted, Eddie was being a saint.

I thought of all the movies Eddie and I had seen together. Probably ninety percent of all the movies I'd seen had been seen with Eddie. We had a history of movies.

Two years from now we'd probably still be seeing movies together and the only difference would be that we'd be in college. Five years from now I'd be putting him through dental school and we'd still be going to the movies. Ten years from now we'd be married and maybe taking our kids to the movies. Was that the purpose of life?

By the time the movie ended, Eddie was asleep. I gave him a push before the lights came up.

"How did it end?" he asked me.

"If you wanted to know, you should've stayed awake," I said, unsure myself how it ended.

"I needed my rest," Eddie said. "I figure you're going to wear me out at the beach party."

I allowed that remark to pass.

The lights came up on his devastating smile. "Hey, Kath, you mad at me?"

"Does it ever seem to you, Eddie, that everything's predictable?"

"Yeah. Most of the time."

"Doesn't that bother you?"

"I find it reassuring."

"You're too young to find it reassuring," I told him, wondering if he found me predictable. "Do you find me boring?" I asked.

"Most of the time.

I was about to punch him when I saw the gleam in his eyes.

We met Jennifer and Alan in the lobby and Jennifer's hair was all messed up. Her lip gloss had disappeared. She told the guys to wait and dragged me into the restroom.

"How'd you like it?" she asked.

"Don't pretend you saw the movie, Jennifer, because I could see you and Alan."

"He is *very* assertive," she said, scowling at me in the mirror while she put about a ton of hair spray on her hair.

Why she was using hair spray when it was going to get all messed up at the beach, I didn't know.

I combed my bangs a little for something to do as I knew how long Jennifer usually took in front of a mirror. "Do you like him?" I asked her.

She made a face. "It's hard to suddenly get excited over someone you've lived across the street from since kindergarten."

"Alan doesn't seem to find it hard."

"Alan could probably get excited over Enid Cortelyou," she said, mentioning the weirdest girl in school.

"Are you going to go out with him again?"

Jennifer shrugged. "Why not? It's not like there's a lot of choice when you're a senior. I can either date Alan, make a play for some younger guy, or start hanging out around the college."

"Maybe a college guy would be a good idea."

"This is the last year we'll all be together," she said. "I'd like to go to all the parties and dances and really have a good time. Anyway, Alan's not that bad. I didn't want to make a scene in the movie, but if he tries anything at the beach party, he's going to have a fight on his hands, believe me."

I didn't believe her. Jennifer was ripe for someone like Alan. Alan's attention was going to make her feel wanted, and she hadn't felt like that since Steve dumped her.

"I shouldn't ask this," Jennifer said, "but would you consider doing me an enormous favor?"

"Sure. You know I would."

"It's just that, well, would you mind kind of sticking around with us at the beach party?"

I was so elated at having an excuse that I could hardly keep from smiling. "I don't mind," I said.

"No, I shouldn't ask. You guys are having your anniversary."

"It's no big deal," I said, as though Eddie wasn't going to kill me if I pulled something like that.

Jennifer gave me a knowing look and I felt myself starting to blush. I was still a little sunburnt from being at the beach earlier, though, so I didn't think she noticed.

We went back to the lobby and the guys were laughing at something but they stopped when they saw us. Before talking to Jennifer, I had it in my mind to suggest we get something to eat before the beach party, even though I was too nervous to eat. Now, however, armed with the perfect excuse to prolong what Eddie thought was going to be the perfect moment, I couldn't wait to get to the beach.

3

Some of the kids were swimming in the ocean even though it's pretty cold out at night in Southern California. Those same kids, though, were probably anticipating being wrapped up in blankets next to warm bodies when they got out. Since I was not anticipating much along those lines, I opted not to go in.

Alan and Eddie were with some of the other guys, gathered around the beer cooler. Jennifer and I were sitting on the sand listening to Lisa go on and on about how she thought she was pregnant and had even gone so far as to tell her mother. Now she was sorry she had because it turned out she wasn't and her mother had imposed a midnight curfew on her. We weren't paying much attention to her because Lisa had periodically thought she was pregnant since seventh grade when she kissed a boy for the first time. Even though she got the same information in sex education that we did, she never seemed to understand it very well.

Personally, I thought Lisa was a virgin.

Mom said that when she was in high school, the girls in her group all lied about being virgins. She said that they all swore they were "saving themselves" for when they got married.

In my group we all claimed that we weren't.

It's not that I lied about it; it's that I let the others assume that Eddie and I had done it. And Eddie, I'm sure, did the same thing. He'd look like a real wimp if his friends thought we hadn't done it, particularly since we'd been going together for so long.

Even though I was so unsure about it, I was on the pill, just in case I decided to give in to Eddie one of these times. But I'd had the foresight not to tell him. He still thought I was worried about getting pregnant.

If it sounds as though I was obsessed with sex, I really wasn't. That was kind of the problem. Everyone else—from my fifteen-year-old brother to my best friend to my boyfriend—seemed to be obsessed with it, and it was beginning to make me feel like a freak. The whole first year Eddie and I had gone out, I'll admit the idea had intrigued me. But now there didn't seem to be any point in going further. I simply wasn't that interested.

Some of the kids started up a volleyball game, although it was too dark to see the ball very well. I said to Jennifer, "Come on, let's play," and pulled her up off the sand. Playing volleyball blind was preferable to listening to Lisa any longer.

As we passed the boys, Eddie said to me, "Have a beer, Kathy—it'll relax you."

I gave him a look to say, *Who do you think you're kidding, Eddie?* which made him laugh.

"I think Alan's getting drunk," said Jennifer, as we walked past them.

I looked back and saw Alan pouring a can of beer over his head. Yeah, I'd say he looked a little drunk. "Don't worry, Eddie's driving," I told her, "and he never gets drunk."

"It's just that if he's drunk, I don't think I'll have any problem with him. He'll probably pass out in the sand and leave me alone."

And I'd be back to having to deal with Eddie. "I'll stick close just in case," I told her. "Anyway, you don't want to end up all alone with a comatose body."

"I don't mind."

"Don't be ridiculous, Jennifer. If he's drunk, we'll leave early, that's all."

"I don't want to spoil your anniversary."

"It's no big deal," I said. "You make it sound like we're married or something."

"Sometimes you two seem that way."

"I know. Isn't it depressing?"

"Depressing?"

"Didn't you ever feel that way with Steve?"

Jennifer shook her head. "Maybe Steve felt that way, and that's why he broke up with me."

Already I was kicking myself for having brought up Steve's name.

We had only been in the volleyball game for five minutes, when Eddie came up behind me and started to wrap my braid around his arm. "Let's take a walk," he suggested in a whisper.

"Where's Alan?" I asked him.

"Swimming."

"He seemed a little smashed to be going swimming."

"Faking being drunk is Alan's way of being the life of the party," said Eddie. He took my hand and we started walking up the beach.

"Let's not go too far," I said.

"Why not?"

"I told Jennifer we'd stick around."

"You *what*?"

"She just doesn't want to be left alone with Alan, that's all."

"Jennifer can take care of herself."

"I'm not so sure. She's feeling rather vulnerable at the moment."

"Jennifer's always feeling vulnerable."

I leaned into Eddie and he put his arm around me and pulled me so close I had trouble walking. "Do you know why Steve broke up with her?" I asked him. He was good friends with Steve and maybe he could solve the puzzle for us. I still didn't think people broke up for no reason.

I could feel Eddie's shrug rather than see it.

"Come on," I said, "there has to be a reason."

"He's dating Marcy McGurn," he said.

"Who's she?" The name sounded familiar but I couldn't place her.

"She used to hang out with your brother's crowd."

"She's a sophomore? Wait a minute. Dark hair? Gigantic boobs?"

Eddie laughed. "That's Marcy."

"Is that why he prefers her? Because she has big boobs?"

"I'm sure there are other considerations," Eddie said, but he was chuckling while he said it.

"Like what?"

"Maybe she's more fun, I don't know. Jennifer always has to make a big production out of everything."

Big boobs. That's all I'd have to tell Jennifer and she'd be truly neurotic. I've always liked being small, but Jennifer swears she's going to get implants when she's twenty-one. By the time she's that old, though, I figure she'll have more sense.

I thought about Marcy McGurn. If she was part of my brother's crowd in junior high, then she was probably one of the kids caught in the skinny-dipping scandal. Seventh graders, and they were having skinny-dipping parties in the school pool after hours. They were all suspended from school over that. One of the conditions of their getting back in school was the breakup of the crowd, but I knew for a fact my brother never stopped being friends with those kids. And knowing Kevin, he was probably one of the ringleaders.

Eddie stopped walking and put his arms around me. We started to kiss and I opened my mouth and his hands began traveling up beneath my sweatshirt. But I couldn't stop thinking about Marcy, and I finally broke off the kiss to say, "Would you break up with me for someone with bigger boobs?"

"I think you have a great body," he said, which was exactly what he was supposed to say.

I was still not quite satisfied, though. "Would you break up with me for someone who's more fun?"

"*You'd* be more fun if you'd quit talking for a minute," Eddie said.

"We need to talk."

"No we don't."

"Yes we do, Eddie."

"You know what we need to do, and it's not talk."

"That's what I want to talk about."

"I don't think I want to hear this." He sat down in the sand and pulled me down beside him.

I moved so that I was leaning across his lap and he had his arms around me. It had always felt good being in Eddie's arms.

"I just don't want to do it yet," I said to him in a small voice.

"Damn it!" he said, getting up so fast my head was dumped in the sand.

I looked up at him. He was standing facing the ocean with his arms crossed. It was too dark to see his expression. "I'm sorry," I said. He hardly ever got angry at me.

"You're always sorry."

"I'm sorry I'm always disappointing you."

"You act like it's a one-way thing here. Like I'm the only one with feelings. Why don't you ever get carried away?"

"I don't let myself," I murmured.

"Well, I'm getting tired of cold showers."

"And I'm getting tired of you always harassing me to do it."

There was dead silence for a moment. "Harassing you? Is that what you call it?"

I was immediately sorry about using that word.

Just because I was abnormal didn't mean I had to take it out on Eddie.

"I can just hear it now. We'll be married ten years and you'll still be saying you don't want to do it yet."

"It won't be that long," I said.

"That's what you told me a year ago." He turned and started to head back in the direction of the party.

"Where are you going?" I asked him.

"I want a beer."

I watched him walk away. I was feeling mixed up and not blaming Eddie at all for wanting to get away from me. I thought of all the other times I'd put him off; each time he had been nice about it, and we'd kissed and made up. But all the other times he could sort of understand my reasons. Nowadays all I could say was, I don't want to.

How could I tell him that I wanted to physically but not emotionally? That I didn't want to take the final step toward ultimate closeness because I wasn't sure he was who I wanted to be ultimately close to? That after two years of nothing being wrong between us, I was having a hard time seeing anything right?

Ugh. I felt that if I had sex with Eddie now, I would be committed to him forever—committed to marrying him and having children with him and putting him through dental school.

Okay, so maybe that's stupid of me. But I'm young. I'm supposed to be stupid.

Anyway, at least things hadn't ended up predictably for once.

4

AFTER ONE WEEK OF SCHOOL I WAS GOING OUT OF my head with boredom. I had all easy classes: chorus, all we did was sing for an hour; English, all we did was read modern American novels; and civics, all we had to do to keep up was watch the news on television. The only class I was getting any homework in was calculus, and that was a snap. I did my calculus homework in homeroom, which left me with nothing to do for my study period.

Last spring, when I had signed up for my classes, having an easy senior year had seemed like a good idea. I had even let Jennifer talk me into taking drama. Well, everything was too easy and too boring except drama, and that was turning out to be my worst nightmare.

The first day wasn't so bad. The class met in the auditorium and we were all sitting there, talking, waiting for the teacher. Then this man walked across the stage and instantly got our attention.

For one thing, he was young. For another, he was rather gorgeous, if you like sleek blonds dressed all in black. Half the class obviously did, and there was a whole lot of sighing going on.

He walked down to the edge of the stage and looked out at us. "I'm Robert Madrigal," he said to us, "but you may call me Robert." His voice was resonant and carried to the last row. I know. That's where I was sitting.

"Robert," I could hear Jennifer whisper in a tone of reverence. An early warning signal that Jennifer was about to fall in love.

He sat down on the edge of the stage and smiled. "Of course that's a stage name, but I've made it legal. And don't ask me what my name used to be because you'll never get it out of me."

He went on to tell us that he was a member of The Actors Studio in New York and was a Method actor. All the kids started buzzing, but I didn't know what he was talking about.

Well, I was soon to find out. We were invited en masse up onto the stage where we had to pretend to be sand crabs. It seemed like very childish behavior to me, but at least we were all involved.

Jennifer was more than involved; she was ecstatic.

Well, anything to take her mind off Steve.

The next day there was a sea of black turtlenecks in the auditorium. I was the only one dressed in jeans and a white cotton sweater. This time we had to go up in groups of three to taste a lemon. Not a real lemon. That wouldn't have been acting. What we were supposed to do was remember what a lemon tasted like, and when we could actually taste it, we could leave the stage.

I couldn't taste it. I could have faked it, I guess, but I didn't. Instead, while the other students came and went, I stayed on the stage for the entire period waiting to taste a lemon.

Jennifer offered to teach me how to taste a lemon after school that day. I turned her down.

The third day we each had to sing a song on stage. Alone. It was supposed to help us overcome any stage fright we might have. Well, I've never seen such a bunch of showoffs as the rest of the class. Each one got up there and belted out a song, and most of them seemed to enjoy it.

I slid down in my seat and hoped to go unnoticed. It didn't work.

"Kathy," Robert said, who had already memorized all our names. "Would you like to give it a try?"

"I'd rather not," I mumbled.

"Go on up," Jennifer said, nudging me. "If you can't think of anything, just sing Jingle Bells."

Where was the earthquake when I needed it?

"Take all the time you need," Robert said.

"She's got a nice voice," offered Jennifer. "She's in chorus with me."

I could've killed her.

"Anytime you're ready," said Robert.

Because I had a long history of obeying authority, I got out of my seat and walked up on stage.

Okay, I told myself, *you'll sing Jingle Bells. It's short, you know all the words, and the worst that can happen is that everyone will laugh at you.*

I was breaking out in a cold sweat and trembling by this point. I opened my mouth and prepared to sing, but nothing came out. My throat actually closed.

Robert finally took pity on me. "Okay, maybe you'll be ready tomorrow," he said to me. "Who wants to be next?"

Without asking permission, I walked down off the stage and right out of the auditorium. I wasn't trying to play hooky or anything, I just wanted out of that class. Permanently. And the only way to do that was to immediately see a guidance counselor.

"What's the problem, Kathy?" Ms. Jackson asked me.

"It's just that . . ." I started to say, then shut my mouth.

"Yes?" she asked.

"Well, I think I made a mistake in one of my course choices," I told her.

She opened up my school record, which was in front of her on the desk. "Which course are you having the problem with?"

"Drama."

"Really? There's someone new teaching that, isn't there?"

"Yes. Mr. Madrigal."

She chuckled. "I've had quite a few girls trying to transfer into that class. He must be young or good-looking or both."

"Both," I said.

"Well, drama isn't a requirement. Do you want to drop it? Take something else?"

"I'd love to."

"I see you originally signed up for physics, then switched to drama."

"That's because my older brother told me I'd flunk it."

"You? With your math grades, it's not likely you wouldn't do well in physics. Don't listen to your brother."

"It wasn't just my brother," I said. Mom had said drama sounded like a lot more fun, and what good would physics ever do me in real life? But Jennifer's argument had probably been the deciding factor. "Why do you want to be in a class full of nerds?" she'd asked me. "Come on, I'm taking drama—we'll ace it." Easy for her to say.

"There's a physics class this period you could transfer to," Ms. Jackson said. "You could go right now. I'll write you a slip to get in."

I started to get a little nervous. Maybe my brother was right. On the other hand, what did he know? I'd always gotten better grades than Mike. He just didn't take me seriously.

"You want me to start *today*?" I asked.

"Why not? You'll only miss about twenty minutes. And you're going to have some catching up to do."

Five minutes later I walked into Mr. Rinaldi's physics class and every nerd in the school turned to look at me. I quickly looked over the class and didn't see any of my friends, which wasn't surprising.

The teacher *was* surprising. He was sitting crosslegged on top of his desk. Now maybe a drama teacher can get away with sitting on the edge of the stage, but this was pretty strange behavior for a regular teacher.

"Is that for me?" he asked, holding out his hand for the slip.

I handed it to him. He must have thought I was a messenger from the office. He studied the transfer for a moment and a look of glee came into his eyes. "Hey, class, we've got a cheerleader joining us," he said, waving the transfer slip in the air.

There was some intellectual chuckling from the nerds. I was so annoyed by his remark that I was ready to walk out of the classroom and head for the parking lot. A whole lot of people assume that because you're not bad-looking, you haven't got a brain in your head. Sometimes you find yourself behaving the way they expect you to behave.

Well, not this time, I decided.

"Actually, I'm taking this class to meet boys," I said coolly, looking over the less-than-wonderful physical specimens filling about two-thirds of the desks. They were smart enough to know I was being sarcastic, and even some of the girls were smirking.

Mr. Rinaldi, however, seemed intent on having fun with me. "I assume you've had the required math courses," he said.

"Of course."

"Do you mean to tell me that lurking beneath the cheerleader exterior is the soul of a physicist?"

Well, I wouldn't exactly go that far. "I guess that will depend on how interesting you make the subject," I said, thinking that the worst that could happen was that I'd be sent to the principal's office for insubordination.

Mr. Rinaldi laughed, and it was a deep rumble that seemed at odds with his impish looks.

He looked at me and raised his eyebrows, giving his face a comical expression. "Ah, a challenge," he said. "I always love a challenge. Take a seat anywhere, Kathy, and stop and see me after class about making up the work you've missed."

The only seats available were in the back row, which was fine with me. Normal students always want to sit in the back. Grinds are another breed entirely.

Several kids gave me disdainful looks as I made my way to the back. I took a seat and got out my notebook. Mr. Rinaldi was asking people questions and I didn't understand what anyone was talking about, so I examined the class instead.

The boys were nothing to look at. Eddie is tall with broad shoulders, brown curly hair, and eyes that are sometimes green and sometimes gray. Along with being very good-looking, he's also smart and fun. Usually. These boys were smart, or at least I assumed so since they were taking physics, but they all looked shorter than me and none of them was memorable. As for being fun, they looked far too serious for that.

With the exception of Enid Cortelyou, I didn't recognize any of the girls. I recognized the type, though: extremely serious. I could tell this by the fact that none of them wore any makeup whatsoever and it looked as though their mothers were still picking out their clothes. And every one of them had a telltale computer squint.

Mr. Rinaldi, though, was younger than any of my other teachers and kind of cute. He had dark hair, worn longer than most of the guys in the school wore theirs. Of course the surfers had long hair, but they had ponytails, while Mr. Rinaldi's was wild and curly. He was wearing a plaid cotton shirt that was open at the neck. No black turtlenecks for him. I wondered if he had been a nerd in high school. He must have grown a few inches in college, traded his glasses for contacts, and learned some social graces. Maybe there was hope for the boys in the class after all.

To kill a little time, I tried a quick make-over of Enid Cortelyou. If she lost a few pounds, used eye makeup on those invisible eyebrows and eyelashes, exchanged her polyester pants for jeans, stood up straight instead of hunching over . . . Sure, and when the earthquake struck, what difference would it make? Anyway, she was so smart she shouldn't have to worry about how she looked. Geniuses are allowed to be different.

Actually there was something about Enid Cortelyou that I had always found scary. There was something mysterious about her, an air of knowing things that other people didn't. Over the years I had been in several classes with her, and though she rarely spoke up, when she did her words always seemed to have hidden meaning. All of this, of course, made her very intimidating, and I wasn't the only one intimidated by her. Teachers never questioned what she said and rarely responded to her. The other kids gave her a wide berth.

I sensed someone's eyes on me and looked up to see Mr. Rinaldi staring at me. He said, "So the thing is, it's impossible to observe reality without changing it."

It took a moment for that to sink in, but when it did, I was really intrigued. I wrote down the words and then stared at them. By observing the words, was I changing them?

"When we're talking about the subatomic realm," he said, and uncrossed his legs to swing them gently in front of his desk, "we can't know both the position and the momentum of a particle with any precision. We can know both approximately, but the more we know about one, the less we know about the other. We can know one precisely, but then we don't know anything about the other. This, guys, is called the Uncertainty Principle." He stood up and wrote it on the crowded blackboard.

The uncertainty principle. I wrote it down too, in my notebook, and fell in love with the words.

I looked up at him and for a moment our eyes met. *Are you a wizard,* I silently asked, *bringing some magic into my life?*

He looked away and I found that for the first time, since maybe second grade, I suddenly couldn't wait to hear what a teacher was going to say next.

5

"**D**ON'T YOU UNDERSTAND?" I SAID TO JENNIFER. "What this means is that right now you could be swallowing the exact same particles that Cleopatra swallowed." I was so excited I could barely concentrate on my driving and a car I had cut off started to put a lot of distance between us.

"Big deal," Jennifer said.

"Don't you find that amazing?"

"What did you say this teacher looked like?" she asked slyly.

"What difference does it make what he looks like? He wasn't the one who came up with the theory."

"You said he's young, right? And cute?"

"Well, appealing. Smart. Enthusiastic and funny."

"Sounds like a winning combination," Jennifer said. "What color are his eyes?"

"Blue," I said without thinking, then, "Oh, come on, Jen. Robert Madrigal is young and cute and I couldn't stand that class another minute."

Jennifer slammed her foot down on the floor-board. "Hey, Kathy, that light's turning—"

"I see it. I was going to stop," I said, quickly applying the brakes. Jennifer tightened her seat belt. "The guidance counselor said lots of girls are trying to transfer into drama."

"Drag. I don't need any more competition."

"Come on, Jen, he's a *teacher*."

"That doesn't mean what it used to mean, Kathy. He's only a few years older than us. Next year it would be *legal* to date him."

A picture of Mr. Rinaldi and me strolling down the beach discussing physics popped into my head. Then I remembered Eddie. What did Eddie and I talk about? I couldn't even remember.

Jennifer said, "So who's in this physics class? Anyone I know?"

"Well, mostly brains."

"There are some really cute guys in drama."

"Give me a break, Jennifer, I'm not looking for boys. I have a boyfriend, in case you haven't no-ticed."

"And the class brain—is she in there?"

"You mean Enid Cortelyou?"

"Of course I mean Enid Cortelyou."

"Yeah, she's in there. Have you ever talked to her?"

"Enid? No one talks to Enid."

"There's something about her I find intriguing."

"She's a robot. It's like someone built a robot and programmed it to be the perfect student. That's Enid Cortelyou."

"I thought the perfect student was supposed to be well-rounded."

"Oh, sure, that's what they tell us, but which do you think teachers prefer? Kids who score one hundred on every test or kids who score seventy and go out for cheerleading?"

"I hope you're right," I said, "since I haven't gone out for anything since freshman year."

"I'm thinking of trying out for the school play," said Jennifer. She looked at me. "Do you think I'm crazy?"

"No. Why not? You'll probably get a part. When are the tryouts?"

"Not for a few weeks. So where are you going? Aren't we going to the mall?" asked Jennifer as I hung a left down her street.

"No, I've got to study. I'm behind in physics and I want to get caught up fast."

"Oh, leave it for the weekend."

"You don't want me to make an idiot of myself in there, do you?"

"This is it? You're just taking me home?"

"Nobody's stopping you from going to the mall."

"In what? My car still isn't fixed. I think the mechanic fell in love with it." She had her hand on the door handle but wasn't opening it. "How about going down to Fatso's for a hamburger?"

"I'm not hungry, Jennifer, and I've really got to study."

"Yeah, okay," she said, opening the door and getting out. "Call me later."

Of course, I felt guilty all the way home. I could've gone to the mall with her, or at least to

Fatso's. It wasn't as though I had to get caught up in one night; Rinaldi had given me a week. But I did hate looking stupid in class, especially a class with all the school brains.

Especially in front of Mr. Rinaldi.

I got home, hoping for some quiet in which to study, but Mom was screaming at Kevin and Kevin was screaming right back. That wasn't a good sign. If Kevin was in trouble again, he would be grounded, which meant Kevin would be hanging around the house being his usual annoying self and getting phone calls every ten seconds from all the girls who were after him.

Kevin wasn't so bad for a fifteen-year-old. At least not nearly as bad as my parents thought he was. If they would just accept the fact that his whole life is surfing, everyone would get along fine. When the big earthquake hits, Kevin is going to be out there surfing the tidal waves.

The screaming stopped when I entered the kitchen. "What's up?" I asked, trying to be casual and hoping to get out of the kitchen without being involved in the argument.

"Well, it's not the surf," my mother said, sounding thoroughly disgusted.

"That's just it, the surf *was* up," Kevin muttered, tying and untying the thong around his ponytail, the way he always does when he's agitated.

I opened the refrigerator and looked inside. The only thing of any interest was a carton of orange juice and I took it out.

"He skipped school again," Mom said, looking at me for support.

I shrugged and poured my orange juice. If I hated school as much as Kevin did, I'd probably ditch, too.

"It's bad enough I've got thirty days after school detention," Kevin said to me, "but now she's grounded me for a month."

Which meant thirty days of a very unhappy Kevin hanging around the house and bothering me. "How was it?" I asked him.

"Great surf."

"It's great surf *every* day in Southern California," Mom said. "What do we have to do, move to another state in order to get you to go to school?"

"Don't bother," Kevin said. "I'm quitting as soon as I'm sixteen anyway."

"Over my dead body," my mother yelled. They began shouting again and I quietly sneaked out of the kitchen and went to my room. It wasn't going to be peaceful at the dinner table at our house that night.

Kevin picked up his lamb chop and started to gnaw at it.

"Please try to eat like a civilized human being," Mom said.

Dad said, "Knock it off, Kevin."

I wished I could pick mine up. It was very hard to get at the meat around the bone. But I wasn't going to start anything now, because I was waiting for the big one. Not the earthquake; the big dinner-table fight.

In an effort to head it off, I said, "I'm taking this class I really like."

My father looked at me. "Just once," he said, "I'd like to hear your brother utter those words."

"I'm sure Mike likes some of his classes," Kevin said. Mike, older than me by three years, is in pre-med.

"I transferred to physics," I said.

"Oh?" Mom said. "Why on earth would you want to take that?"

"Do you even know what it is?" I asked her.

"Don't talk to your mother that way," said my father.

"Of course I know what it is," she said. "I just don't know why you want to waste your time with it."

"How can it be a waste of time for me to get some education?" I asked.

"Kathy!" Dad yelled. "I don't want to hear you use that tone of voice with your mother."

Some parents would be thrilled to have a daughter who was smart and did well in school. Not mine. I decided to shut up and let Kevin take the heat, which was not long in coming.

"Your youngest son skipped school again today," my mother informed my father.

"Look, I'm already getting punished by the school," said Kevin. "I don't think it's fair that I'm getting punished at home, too."

"I've grounded him for a month," Mom said.

Dad made a production out of putting down his knife and fork and sighing. "What did I tell you would happen if you ditched school again, Kevin?" he asked.

"I don't remember," Kevin muttered.

"Well, let me refresh your memory. I believe I said I'd withdraw your college fund from the bank and invest it in something more profitable."

Kevin said, "Do what you want, it's your money."

"I'm talking about your future, young man!"

"I don't want to go to college. I don't even want to go to high school."

"And just how do you expect to support yourself when you're an adult? Your older brother's going to be a doctor. What are *you* going to be?"

"I don't even know what *I'm* going to be," I said, but everyone ignored me.

"I'm going to be a surfer," Kevin said.

"Oh yes, lots of money in that," my father said.

"There are other things in life besides money, Dad," said Kevin sarcastically.

"Yes, but they don't put food on the table," Dad said, "and I notice you're not doing without."

"Keep your food," Kevin said, getting up from the table and stomping out of the room.

I was sorry he beat me to it. I had been about to excuse myself, but now I'd have to wait a few minutes until things died down. I sighed quietly and pushed food around on my plate.

"*Surfing,*" my father said in disgust, pushing his plate away as though he'd lost his appetite.

"I really don't know what to do with him anymore," Mom said. "The school is on the phone to me every day."

"He's not the only one," I said.

"I beg your pardon?" my mother said.

"All the surfers ditch school when the surf's good. It's not just Kevin."

"Well, he's the only one I'm responsible for," she said.

"Maybe you could talk to your brother," Dad said.

"*Me?* He never listens to me."

"Give it a try, Kathy, okay?" Mom said.

Sometimes all I seemed to be in the family was a go-between.

After dinner I knocked on my brother's door. When he didn't answer, I opened the door a little and stuck his dessert plate through the opening. "It's chocolate cake," I said.

"In that case, come on in," Kevin said.

He was sitting on his bed watching a surfing movie. That's the only thing he ever watches on TV and the only kind of movies he ever goes to. Surfers are weird.

"What is this, a bribe so I'll talk to you?"

I nodded and sat down in his desk chair. His desk was the cleanest spot in the room since he never studied.

"Whatever you're going to say, I'm sure I've heard it before."

"Just eat your dessert," I said.

He dug right in. Next to surfing, Kevin loves chocolate better than anything.

Kevin looks exactly like me. Well, not exactly, I mean he *is* a boy. We've both got the same thick, straight, reddish brown hair, only he wears his tied back with a thong and I usually braid mine. We both have eyes the color of dark coffee and the

McKenna nose, which means small, and mouth, which means big. We're both tall and slim but he's taller than I am. The comparison ends there, though. Kevin has a single-minded interest in surfing and all I have are a lot of little interests that don't amount to much. I was sorry that I didn't have something like surfing to pour all my energies into.

"Well, let's take ditching school to its logical conclusion," I said.

Kevin looked up from the cake and rolled his eyes.

"First the school will suspend you, right?"

Kevin shrugged.

"And then they'll expel you."

"You think I care?"

"And then, since you're not sixteen and legally still have to be in school, you'll get sent to reform school somewhere. As far as I know, there aren't any reform schools at the beach. Which means no surfing."

"They're not going to send me to reform school."

"Yes, they will, they'll have to," I said. "First it will be Juvenile Hall, then reform school. I've heard of kids it's happened to."

"Dad isn't going to let me go to reform school. He'd send me to a private school first."

"Sure," I said. "A military academy. You think you're going to do much surfing there?"

"I'd run away, that's all."

He had an answer for everything. I got up and headed for the door. "Don't say I didn't try," I said to him.

"Thanks for the cake," he said.

I went to my room, took my phone off the hook, and opened my physics book. I was afraid that the textbook wouldn't be as interesting as the class, that maybe it was Mr. Rinaldi I found interesting and not the subject. But I got hooked pretty quickly. I kept underlining things I liked and then going back and reading them again. It was better than science fiction. I didn't understand everything I read, but maybe Mr. Rinaldi could explain it to me after class. I felt like killing my older brother for telling me not to take it.

It was like being let in on all these secrets that I wanted to hang on to, yet at the same time I wanted to tell everyone else about them. I had the urge to go downstairs and tell my parents about it, but I knew they wouldn't listen. Kevin certainly wouldn't, and Jennifer would manage to change the subject. Eddie would listen to me, but only to humor me.

I was deep into a fantasy of Mr. Rinaldi tutoring me privately when there was a knock on my door and Mom stuck her head in.

"Do you have your phone off the hook?" she asked me.

"I'm studying."

"Well, Eddie called and wants you to call him."

"Yeah, okay."

When she closed the door, I dialed his number. He picked up on the first ring.

"Who've you been talking to for the past hour?" he asked. "Jennifer?"

"No, I took it off the hook so I could study. I

dropped drama today and switched to physics. I think I really like it. You had it last year, didn't you?"

"All year."

"Did you have the uncertainty principle? Isn't it wonderful?"

"Well, let me tell you, Kath. Wonderful is the certainty you're going to catch a touchdown pass; wonderful is not the uncertainty principle."

"Okay, but you have to admit it's intriguing."

"Intriguing is the thought of when I'm finally going to get you to—"

"I don't want to hear it, Eddie!"

"I can't even *talk* about it?"

"No. Eddie? Do you ever wish that everything in your life wasn't so predictable?"

"You asked me that before."

"I know, but I'm still thinking about it."

"That's what I like about football, it's never predictable."

"Am I predictable?"

"Always. But I still love you."

"Maybe one of these days I'll stop being so predictable."

"When? When?"

"I don't mean *that*, Eddie."

"And here you got me all excited."

"Good night, Eddie."

6

MANDY JENSEN WAS GIVING HER FIRST PARTY OF THE year after the football game and Eddie wanted to go since the rest of the team would be there. I wasn't really up for it. First of all, Mandy had been giving parties since seventh grade and they were always the same: soft drinks by the pool; snacks in the living room; and her parents relentlessly hovering to make sure we either had a good time, which is what *they* said, or behaved ourselves, which is what *I* thought.

Also, Jennifer had decided not to go, and if she wasn't going, I wouldn't have anyone to talk to while Eddie was celebrating (or commiserating) with his buddies.

The party was going strong by the time we arrived. Everything was just as I had pictured it except the people. Mandy's a senior, too, and usually it was mostly our classmates at her parties. This year, though, with the exception of Mandy and myself, most of the girls were younger and some of them I didn't even recognize.

It shouldn't have surprised me. I knew that a lot of the senior girls were dating college guys, which meant the senior boys were now dating younger girls. Still, it seemed weird to see all those cute young things. It made me feel old.

Another surprise was seeing Steve there with a cute little bombshell who, judging by Eddie's description, had to be Marcy McGurn. I had to admit she had a pretty spectacular figure for a sophomore and just about all of it was showing in her bikini top and miniskirt. Steve and several other boys appeared to be drooling over her. I was glad Jennifer wasn't there to see it.

We had won the game, so Eddie was in a good mood. He joined the rest of the team about two seconds after we arrived. I grabbed a Coke and hunted up Mandy.

"Who *are* all these people?" I asked her.

"Beats me," said Mandy. "I invited the same people I always invite, but a lot of girls couldn't come and most of the boys brought girls I've never seen before."

"And we're going to have to go through all this again in college," I said.

"All what?"

"Oh, starting off being the youngest ones at the parties; the new girls. And then by the time we're seniors, most of the girls our age will probably be married, and there will be all these younger girls again."

"You and Eddie probably will be married," she said.

"I guess," I agreed, unable to show any enthusiasm for the idea. Married. For life. To a dentist.

She must have picked up on it because she asked, "Things okay between you and Eddie?"

"Oh, sure. What about you and Mark?"

"Things are fine with us."

"You'll probably get married before we do," I said. They hadn't been dating as long as Eddie and I had, but they'd been hot and heavy for over a year now.

Mandy shook her head. "We're breaking up at the end of the year."

"Are you serious?" I couldn't help admiring her for being so calm about it. Whenever I really thought about breaking up with Eddie, I got so worried about what I would do with myself that I always changed my mind.

Mandy was continuing, "He wants to go to Stanford and I'm going east to college. There doesn't seem any point in still going together. I know I wouldn't trust him, and I'd probably want to date, anyway. Are you and Eddie still planning on UCLA?"

I nodded. "We've applied there, anyway. And I can't see any reason why we wouldn't be accepted. Mandy, what are you going to go for in college?"

"You mean my major? Psychology. I think I'd like to work with disturbed children."

"When did you decide that?"

"Last spring, when I was doing some volunteer

work at the hospital. What about you? You decided on a major yet?"

"No. Everyone else knows what they want to do. Eddie's going to be a dentist like his dad, Jennifer wants to major in drama ... I don't know, I just wish I knew what I was going to do."

"Well, you can always be a dentist's wife," said Mandy.

"You sound just like my mother." I grimaced.

A few minutes later I noticed that Eddie had wandered off and I went in search of him. I found him by the pool talking to Steve and surrounded by bikini-clad beach bunnies, looking about fourteen and gazing at him with adoring eyes. Give me a break. They made a path for me when they saw me approaching, and one of them said, "Wasn't Eddie marvelous in the game tonight?"

"Which play are you referring to?" I asked her, pinning her down with my eyes.

She looked a little flustered. "Well, when he caught that ball," she said, sounding proud of the fact that she knew what a catch was.

"In which quarter?" I asked. Being a wide receiver, Eddie had caught several passes that night.

Ignoring the question, she said, "I think he's wonderful," and her eyes resumed their adoring gaze.

Eddie wasn't falling for this crap, was he? I felt a momentary twinge of—I don't know. I guess it *was* jealousy. I groaned inwardly. What was wrong with me? If I didn't want him, why was I jealous? If I did want him, why didn't I *want* him? I must be nuts.

* * *

"Hi, Kathy," said Steve.

"How're you doing?" I asked him.

He looked a little embarrassed, and no wonder, with Marcy climbing all over him. "Hanging in there," he said, which got a giggle from Marcy.

I grabbed Eddie's hand and said, "Hey, you want to dance?"

He nodded and I led him over to the patio where slow music was playing and a few couples were pretending to dance. As soon as he wrapped his arms around me, I whispered in his ear, "Let's cut out of here." I felt like I needed some time alone with him.

"What've you got in mind?" he whispered back.

"This is boring. I'll be glad when we don't have to go to high school parties anymore."

"I think it's about to stop being boring," he said, turning us around so I could see who had just arrived at the party.

"Oh, no," I said. Jennifer and Alan were coming through the sliding glass doors. As far as I knew, she hadn't even had a date tonight and was mad because I wouldn't miss the game and go to the movies with her. Also as far as I knew, this would be the first time she had met up with Steve in public since he dumped her. I hoped she wasn't going to make a scene, but I knew that Jennifer was quite capable of it, and a dramatic one at that.

"Do you think we ought to head them off before she sees him?" I asked Eddie.

"What's she going to do, drown him in the pool?"

"Possibly."

"Nah, I gotta see this," said Eddie.

"Well, if Alan and Steve get into anything—"

"Steve's not going to get in a fight over Jennifer," said Eddie. "In fact, I've never known Steve to get into a fight over anything."

"Would you get into a fight if I came to the party with someone else?" I still felt a little weird about Eddie's adoring fan.

"That's different. I'd kill the guy."

"I don't see the difference," I said.

"You're mine," he said.

I decided to ignore his delusion. "Did I tell you about the particles?"

"Yeah, you told me."

"Just think, right now you could have the same particles in your body that were once in Napoleon's body."

"I have an idea, Kath. Why don't I put some of my particles into your body?"

"Forget it, Eddie!"

"I was just talking about kissing."

"Sure you were."

"It's you with the dirty mind, Kathy, not me. I swear, that was a perfectly innocent remark."

He leaned down and kissed the tip of my nose and I smiled. I have to hand it to him—sometimes he can be very cute. Then I saw that Jennifer had spotted Steve and her usually rosy cheeks were slowly turning purple.

"I'll be right back," I said to Eddie, practically running down a couple of dancers in my haste to get to Jennifer.

She saw me a split second before I grabbed her arm.

"Hey, Jen," I said. "I'm glad you're here."

"Who's that little tramp he's with?" she hissed.

"Oh, ah, she's a sophomore," I said. "I think she knows my brother."

"What's the child's name?"

"Hey, she's only two years younger than us," I said. "Calm down."

"I asked you her name."

"Uh, I think it's Marcy McGurn."

"Couldn't she find a bikini any smaller?" she asked, but she already knew the answer to that one. If Marcy could have, she would have.

"Hi, Alan," I said, looking past Jennifer and seeing the amusement on his face.

"Kathy."

"Hey," I said brightly. "Eddie and I were just leaving to get something to eat. Why don't you guys go with us?"

Alan was just opening his mouth to answer when Jennifer took off in the direction of Steve and Marcy. By this time most of the kids were aware of what was going on and were watching avidly to see what would happen.

"Stop her, Alan," I said.

"And miss all the fun?" he asked.

Then I heard Jennifer say, "Who's the little tramp you're with, Steve?"

"Take it easy, Jen," said Steve.

"Introduce me to your girlfriend," she insisted.

Steve was looking around, trying to judge the situation. Marcy was eating it up. Seeing that Steve wasn't going to introduce her, she introduced herself. "I'm Marcy," she said to Jennifer.

"Marcy McGurn?" asked Jennifer in a deadly voice.

"That's right," said Marcy, wriggling in enjoyment at all the attention she was getting.

Jennifer gave her a deceptively sweet smile. "The same Marcy McGurn who got thrown out of junior high for carrying on in the school pool?"

There was dead silence for about six seconds. Then Marcy said, "I guess you heard about us," and Jennifer said, "I think everyone's heard about you." The next thing that happened was that Jennifer shoved Marcy into the pool. This was quickly followed by a round of applause, Mandy's parents coming out of the house to see what was happening, and Marcy losing the top of her bikini trying to get out of the pool.

Jennifer stalked up to me, Eddie, and Alan, saying, "Let's blow this joint," and that was when we all left the party.

We had no sooner ordered hamburgers at Fatso's than Jennifer dragged me off to the ladies' room. Once inside, she leaned against the door so no one else could come in, and said, "Now you know why he dumped me."

"I don't think he was seeing her before you two broke up," I said.

"There's only one reason why a boy goes out with someone with her reputation."

"Not Steve," I said.

"Yes, Steve," she said, nodding.

"But why would he—"

"For *sex*. What else?"

"But he already had you," I said, not understanding.

Jennifer's cheeks began to turn purple again. "I wouldn't let him," she muttered.

"*What?*"

"I feel really stupid telling you this, Kathy, but we never did it."

"You're still a virgin? You've been lying to me?"

She nodded, avoiding my eyes. "What can I tell you? I felt stupid. I mean, everyone else was doing it."

"We're not," I blurted out.

"You're just saying that to make me feel better," said Jennifer, dismissing my confession.

"No, I'm not," I said. "I feel pretty stupid about it, too. The whole thing is embarrassing. I'm such an idiot."

"I don't believe this for a minute. This is inconceivable." Jennifer started to laugh.

"Eddie thinks so, too." I couldn't help smiling.

"Don't tell me we're the last two virgins left in Huntington Beach High School."

"Well, there's always Enid Cortelyou."

"She doesn't count, but I was sure you and Eddie . . ."

"Yeah, well, he's not thrilled about it. And he's stepping up the pressure."

"So was Steve. He gave me an ultimatum, and when I said no, he dumped me."

"Oh, you're kidding. What a jerk." Jennifer nodded. I wondered if Eddie was going to dump me soon, too.

I started to laugh. "Did you see Marcy's top fall off?"

"How could you tell?" said Jennifer. "It looked off to me when it was on."

"She's got a cute little figure."

"*Little?* You call that *little*? I'd die for *half* of what she's got."

"Well, let's go eat before the guys come and drag us out of here. Maybe you'll put a little weight on."

"Yeah, on my thighs. Never where I want to put it."

We were at Fatso's for about an hour and I could tell that Jennifer was starting to like Alan. I think at first she only went out with him because there wasn't anyone else to go out with, but now, by the way she was enjoying arguing with him, I could tell there was an attraction. I hoped so, 'cause she sure wasn't going to get Steve back after what she pulled tonight.

"Eddie!"

"What? Shhhh."

"Stop it, Eddie!"

"Oh, Kathy . . ."

"I mean it!" I pushed him off me and sat up in the sand. "I thought you wanted to run on the beach."

"We ran."

"Yeah, about ten yards."

"You're driving me nuts, you know that?"

"I don't mean to drive you nuts, Eddie, I just—" I brushed sand off my hands to buy some time.

"What? You just what?" Eddie said tightly. I

looked at him. He was lying on his back in the sand, his hands clasped behind his head. He looked young, healthy, in the prime of life, and very angry.

"Eddie," I began. He didn't say anything. "I love you," I said.

"I find that hard to believe."

"I do. I always have. I just—I just don't know how committed I want to be right now ..." I said in a small voice.

Eddie sat up. "Jesus, Kathy. We've been going steady for *two years*. All of a sudden you don't feel committed? Aren't we planning to go to UCLA? Aren't we planning on living together? Was I just *dreaming* all this?"

Uncharacteristically I felt like I might start crying.

"Was I?"

"No." I sniffed.

"Look. You want to break up?"

"No." I didn't *think* I did. I didn't know.

"Kathy." He shuffled closer and put his arms around me. I still liked the way that felt. He kissed my neck. Without butter and salt, it wasn't too bad.

"Let's just play it by ear," he said. "We'll just relax and take it easy." I nodded.

"And if you don't sleep with me soon, I'm going to absolutely kill you," he whispered romantically. I couldn't help giggling. I picked up some sand and held it. "I suppose you tell everyone that we do it."

"Why should I do that?"

"I don't know. To sound macho, I guess."

"I don't lie about it," he said. I was really surprised.

"Not even in the locker room?"

"Those guys are making bets on how much longer you can hold me off."

I smiled. Where would I ever find a guy that I could trust as much as Eddie?

"I don't mind if you lie to them."

"I wouldn't lie about something like that. And when it happens, I'm not going to walk into the locker room and announce it, either. How childish do you think I am?"

"I've been lying," I said.

"What?"

"Well, not exactly lying, but not saying we haven't, either."

"That's probably really confusing the guys."

"So that's why Steve's going with Marcy, huh?"

"That's what it looks like."

"Maybe I'll give you a hot little sophomore for your birthday."

"I wouldn't complain."

I threw some sand in his face and he let out a howl. Then I was up and running.

7

KEVIN FINALLY BLEW IT.

It was a normal dinner until Dad mentioned that when he was driving home from work he had seen enormous waves washing up on the beach, waves almost as high as the pier. He said there were police there keeping people off the beach.

Kevin suddenly started gobbling down his dinner as though he really liked lamb stew. Then he quickly excused himself from the table, saying, "I've got to go by Jeff's house and study for a test with him."

I, of course, didn't believe this for a minute. I was smart enough to connect his sudden appetite with the news about the waves, plus Kevin had never studied for a test in his life.

Mom, though, looked at Kevin as though she was really pleased, and even Dad told him to run along. I guess he wasn't grounded as long as he was going to "study."

When I finished eating, I said I thought I'd go

down and see the waves. Dad said he'd go down with me, so we got into my car and headed for the pier.

The waves *were* awesome, and I could understand that they would seem magical to Kevin. By this time they were going right over the pier in spots, almost like a tidal wave from an earthquake. I could feel their power as they crashed into shore and wondered if Kevin saw his destiny in each monstrous wave.

We weren't the only ones down there to see it— the parking lot was packed with people. Dad and I got out of the car and walked as close to the pier as we were allowed to. That's when we saw the kids surfing. The police kept yelling at them to get out of the water, but the kids kept riding the high waves in.

Some of the people were cheering them on. There was something heroic about those kids matching their skill against the forces of nature.

The police helicopters came in from the north, hovering low over the pier and yelling through bullhorns for the surfers to go ashore for their own safety. I thought I recognized Kevin out there, but I wasn't sure. Oh, I was sure he was one of them, all right, I just wasn't sure which one. I didn't tell Dad, though, because he would've blown a fuse.

The blown fuse came a couple of hours later when Kevin called from the police station wanting Dad to come down and get him out. Dad told him that as far as he was concerned, Kevin could stay in jail for the duration of the school year. As a result, Kevin was taken to Juvenile Hall.

Later that night, I overheard Dad telling Mom

that he thought a good, strict boarding school might be just the thing for Kevin. I didn't hear what Mom said, but she probably agreed.

The next morning Kevin was the talk of the school. Everyone else's parents had made bail and Kevin, the only one to be taken to Juvenile Hall, was now some kind of hero to his friends. Boys with long hair kept coming up to me and asking about Kevin, and quite a few girls did, too. They all seemed to think it was cool. My friends had also heard about it, but they were stopping me in the halls to say they were sorry. I didn't like all the attention I was getting from my notorious younger brother.

It was a relief to go to physics class. I had been looking forward to it all morning. Surfers didn't take things like physics, nor did their girlfriends, and I could be reasonably certain that no one in there would have heard about Kevin.

Mr. Rinaldi, wearing tan canvas pants and a blue shirt, was busying himself at his desk when I walked in. The class seemed on edge. Or maybe I was the one on edge and was projecting it onto the class. Or maybe they knew something I didn't know, which turned out to be the case. Rinaldi stood up, announced, "We're going to have a quiz, guys," then went to the board and began to write out the questions.

The others already had paper and pencils out, so I quickly tore out a couple of sheets of notebook paper and found my one pencil that still had a point.

My stomach tightened up. I didn't recongnize it

because I wasn't used to feeling nervous about tests. With all the excitement last night I hadn't gotten any reading done, though, and had reason to be nervous.

The first five test questions were okay. They pertained to information we had either covered since I'd been in class or I had read about on my own. They were essay questions and I took my time answering them, using up the two pieces of paper I had taken out and taking out several more.

The last five questions were a different story. They were on information I hadn't read about or even heard about. For a few moments I panicked; then I realized I found them interesting. I read the questions carefully, applied a little logic, and let my imagination soar. This seemed strange since I had never thought of myself as being imaginative. Something about the questions made me come up with my own ideas on subjects I knew nothing about. It was like solving a puzzle.

I was off in my own world with Rinaldi called for our papers to be passed up. It took a real effort to finish the sentence I was working on and hand it in. Ideas were coming at me so fast I felt as though I could keep writing forever.

There was a lot of grumbling after the tests were passed in. Richard McKenzie, whom I've been in school with since kindergarten and who I think had his first chemistry set when he was still in a crib, was grumbling the loudest, telling Rinaldi it wasn't fair to quiz us on stuff we hadn't had yet in class.

Rinaldi, cross-legged on his desk and looking unperturbed, smiled out at us. "I just wanted to see what kind of brains we *really* have in here," he said. I was struck again by how young he looked. He looked almost as young as Robert Madrigal. But not nearly as pretentious.

Enid Cortelyou muttered something, but no one could tell what she said.

"Yes, Enid?" asked Mr. Rinaldi.

Enid shook her head and lowered it.

"Did you have a problem with the test, Enid?" Mr. Rinaldi asked her.

"No, sir," she mumbled.

"That's what I thought," said Rinaldi. Then he looked at me in the back row and a gleam came into his eyes. This was the first quiz we had had since I had joined the class. "And what did our cheerleader think of the quiz?"

There was the usual sniggering. Since I'd seen Rinaldi at the football game, I knew that he knew I wasn't a cheerleader, so I let that remark pass.

"It was okay," I said.

"Just okay? Nothing else?"

"I found it interesting."

He beamed at me. "Did any of the rest of you find it interesting?" he asked.

There wasn't one hand raised. Great. Now when I flunked it, they'd really laugh at me.

"Well, I'm glad you found it interesting, Kathy," said Rinaldi. "I hope I find what you wrote just as interesting."

I was a little miffed that Rinaldi had singled me out like that, but then he began to teach us something so wonderful that I forgot I was annoyed and once again fell under his blue-eyed spell.

* * *

"You're not listening to me," I said, ignoring the lunch on my tray.

"This isn't lunchtime conversation, Kathy," said Jennifer. "Boys are lunchtime conversation. Clothes are lunchtime conversation. Physics is not lunchtime conversation."

"Okay, let me explain it another way."

"Please don't," said Jennifer.

"Then listen to this. When you're driving down Pacific Coast Highway, your car is shorter than it is when it's sitting in your driveway. And it weighs less. And if you're wearing a watch while you're driving, your watch is running more slowly than when it's sitting on your dresser."

"Assuming I believe that, Kath, and I'm not sure I do," she said in a low voice, looking around as though she hoped no one was going to overhear our conversation, "the thing is, who cares?"

"Don't you find it fascinating?"

"Your brother is in Juvenile Hall. That I find fascinating. Do you suppose your father has gotten him out?"

"Just one more thing."

Jennifer groaned.

"If you're flying and you stand up in the aisle and face the cockpit, you're thinner than if you faced the other direction."

Jennifer rolled her eyes. "If I were fat and flying somewhere that might be interesting. Right here, right now, it just isn't."

Of course it wasn't interesting to her and I knew it wouldn't be. I was sure she'd find my growing fascination with Rinaldi a lot more interesting, but physics was easier to talk about.

"I don't know," I said.

"I don't know either."

"No, I mean I don't know if Kevin's still locked up. I do know my father stayed home from work, though."

"Well, maybe you'll get your wish and become an only child."

"I don't wish I was an only child. I just wish my parents would pay more attention to me."

"Start cutting school to go surfing and maybe they will."

She was wrong, though. They wouldn't. My parents felt that school wasn't as important for girls as it was for boys. The fact that I did better in school than my brothers hadn't changed their minds. It was so stupid. Even though I didn't know what I wanted to do with my life, I did know that being Betty Crocker wasn't a goal I was comfortable with.

"So," said Jennifer, "are we going to the mall after school?"

"I want to go to the public library and check out some books."

"What for?"

"I want to get some books on physics, that's all."

"You're really getting weird, Kathy. I can't believe you'd rather go to the library than to the mall."

"I'll still drive you home."

"Never mind. I'll get Alan to go with me."

"Which reminds me, any flak about Mandy's party?"

Jennifer looked smug. "Pushing Marcy into the pool was one of the smartest things I've ever done."

"Did Steve break up with her?"

"Oh, no. At least not that I've heard. But people have been coming up to me all day and congratulating me. It seems little Marcy isn't so well liked."

"People have been coming up to me all day about Kevin. I think my brother's better known in this school than I am."

"Yes, but for the wrong reasons."

"True."

When I got home from the library, my well-known brother was there. So were my parents. I could sense a battle had been fought and now an uneasy truce was in effect.

"Hey, Kevin," I said, skirting the living room where they were seated. This looked serious. We generally didn't use the living room for anything.

"Hey, Kath," he said, then rolled his eyes a little.

I was heading for the stairs when my father said, "Kathy, would you please come in here?"

I set my library books on the hall table and went into the living room. Mom and Dad were seated in the chairs on either side of the fireplace. Kevin, rather upright for him, was on the couch. I sat at the other end.

"So what's up?" I said.

"This isn't funny, Kathy," said Dad. "Your brother's in serious trouble."

"Is he going to reform school?" I asked, and saw that Kevin was trying not to laugh.

"Please, Kathy," said Mom.

"We've decided to give your brother one last chance before we ship him off to military school," my father said.

"Well, good," I said.

My father gave me an exasperated look. "The game plan, Kathy, is for you to drive your brother to school and home every day."

"Yeah, okay. I don't mind giving him a ride."

"Obviously you can't watch him every minute of the day," said Mom, "but you can make sure he actually gets to school in the morning and doesn't go anywhere afterward."

I glanced over at Kevin but couldn't read his expression.

"He's grounded," said my father. "Permanently."

"You mean he can't even surf on weekends?" I asked.

"No surfing until further notice," said my father.

I looked at Kevin. I could see by the look in his eyes that it was never going to work.

8

A DEFEATED-LOOKING ENID CORTELYOU WAS ALL hunched up over her desk. The results of the quiz had just been announced and I was the only one to get a perfect score.

Rinaldi, cross-legged on his desk as usual, had called out each name and announced the test score. When he reached my name, he looked at me, lifted his eyebrows, and wiggled them for a moment, then said, "Kathy was the only one who answered every question, if not correctly, at least in an innovative way. After all, sometimes in physics there is no right or wrong, just a lot of hotly contested theories."

There was dead silence in the room and I was wishing for at least a minor earth tremor.

"Kathy," he said to me, "please see me after class."

What made my test results more amazing was the fact that some of the biggest brains in the class flunked it.

Enid Cortelyou got the next highest score, but she was five points behind me. Other kids were shooting me suspicious looks and doubtful looks and there were even a couple of congratulatory looks from girls who probably thought Rinaldi picked on me too much. But Enid's despair was beginning to unnerve me.

Maybe she thought it was unfair. I had all the things she didn't have: friends, a boyfriend, a social life, etcetera, and then I beat her at the one thing she did have. Not that it would probably ever happen again. And not that the things I had made me feel happier and more worthwhile. Anyway, I didn't know the answers to those questions either, so it was no doubt a fluke that I got them right.

Despite Enid, however, I was thrilled. Thrilled that I had somehow improved my image and thrilled that Mr. Rinaldi wanted to see me after class. I wondered if he would look at me in a new way now; whether I had gained some measure or respect in his eyes. It felt good thinking that at least one person thought I was special because of how I thought, rather than what I looked like or if I was fun.

I stared down at my notebook and tried to think about something unpleasant so I wouldn't smile. A smile would look smug to the rest of the class.

That's when I got my bright idea. I guess beating Enid on the quiz made me feel benevolent toward her, because I started to think, *Wouldn't it be nice if someone asked Enid Cortelyou to the Homecoming Dance?*

I had been in school with Enid since seventh

grade and not once had I seen her at a party or a dance. I didn't recall even seeing her at a movie. She moved through the halls at school as though she were invisible, never talking to anyone, never having anyone talk to her. She even spent her lunch hour alone.

Everyone told us we were supposed to be well-rounded. Well, Enid wasn't well-rounded. But maybe I could rectify that.

After class I stopped at Mr. Rinaldi's desk. When he gave me a questioning look, I said, "You wanted to see me?" I liked being this close to him. I liked being able to see the clear blue of his eyes and the laugh lines that fanned out from each corner.

"I haven't seen you at physics club," he said.

"I didn't know there was one," I said, disappointed that this was all he had wanted to see me about.

"I think it might interest you. You seem to have been doing some reading on your own, which leads me to believe you like the subject."

"I love it," I said, smiling. And I like the way you teach it, I thought.

"We meet after school on Fridays for an hour."

I had to wait around an hour for Kevin to finish his after-school detention anyway, so I told him I'd come. And then I confessed, "I don't really know how I got an A on that test. On the last part of it I didn't even know what I was talking about."

"I know," he said, "but you were theorizing and your mind was going in some interesting directions. And that's mainly what physicists do."

"So my answers were right?"

"There wasn't really a right or wrong. I just wanted to see what you guys could come up with. You came up with the most interesting theories."

"Thanks," I said, basking in the glow. He found me interesting.

"Thank *you*. It's always rewarding when you can interest a student in your subject."

I practically floated out of his classroom. He would never know how hard I had worked to get that kind of approval from him.

When the fourth guy from physics passed by our lunch table and said hi to me, Jennifer gave me a quizzical look. "Is there something I should know about?" she asked.

"I think it's because I got an A on a quiz Rinaldi gave us."

"You always get A's."

"Yes, but I was the only one who got one."

"You mean the *brains* flunked it? How about Enid Cortelyou?"

"No, she didn't flunk it, but I scored better than she did. She spent the rest of the class in a funk. Which reminds me. I was thinking about Enid during class. I think it would be nice if someone asked her to the Homecoming Dance."

"It would be nice if it snowed in Southern California, too, but it's not going to happen."

"Surely we can think of someone who would ask her."

"Keep dreaming."

* * *

"Can't you just drive by the pier?" Kevin begged from the backseat. "It's not going to kill you just to drive by."

Jennifer and I exchanged looks in the front seat. "Go on," she said, "give him a thrill."

"You're supposed to go right home after detention, Kevin," I said.

"Five minutes isn't going to hurt."

"How much do you want to see the pier, Kevin? Enough to do me a favor in return?"

"Depends on the favor."

"Tell me, Kevin, do you have a date for the Homecoming Dance?"

Jennifer burst out laughing.

"What's so funny?" Kevin asked.

"Don't pay any attention to her," I said. "Just answer the question."

"No, I haven't asked anyone. But I'll probably take Susie."

"Ask him, I dare you," said Jennifer.

"Ask me what?"

"If I drive by the pier for you, Kevin, will you ask a girl in one of my classes to the dance?"

"What kind of a reputation does she have?"

"She's the smartest girl in the school," said Jennifer.

"Then why would she want to go out with me?"

"Never mind, Kevin," I said. "Forget I mentioned it."

"Does that mean we don't go by the pier?"

"See, you're pretty smart yourself."

* * *

"What's that supposed to be?" asked Jennifer, looking at the large black letters I had printed in the center of my formerly blank white wall.

"You don't know what $E=mc^2$ means?" I asked.

"No."

"It's the formula for Einstein's theory of relativity."

"Like we really learned that in drama."

I stood in the doorway of my room for a moment, gazing at the formula. I was in love with it.

"Couldn't you just hang a picture of Sting on the wall?"

"I like this better. You know what we learned in class today?"

She turned around and folded her arms. "Kathy, it's bad enough you pressured me into coming over here and helping you find Enid a date. I'm not going to listen to physics, too."

I took last year's yearbook out of my bookcase and handed it to her. "Here, make a list of likely candidates."

"There's no such thing," she said, but she sat down on my bed and started looking through it.

"Aren't there any boys who owe you a favor?"

"Yes. Alan. But *I'm* going to the dance with him."

"Hey, Kathy?"

I looked up and saw Kevin at the door. "What do you want?"

He slinked into the room. "What you asked me before. About asking some girl to the dance? Maybe we could make a deal."

"I can't wait to hear this," said Jennifer.

Kevin glanced over at Jennifer and then back at me.

"Could we talk alone?"

"Whatever is it, Jennifer's not going to go blabbing it."

"One day of surfing, that's all I ask."

"You mean ditch school for an entire day?"

Kevin nodded. "And forging me a note the next day."

"Sorry, Kevin."

"You won't get another offer like that," said Jennifer.

"A half a day?" Now he was bargaining.

"I can't do it, Kevin. I promised Mom and Dad, and if you got caught, you'd be in military school and I'd be grounded."

"Thanks a lot," he said, storming out of my room and slamming the door behind him.

"You should've taken him up on it," said Jennifer. "He's going to ditch school one of these days, anyway, and there's nothing you're going to be able to do about it."

"Well, I'm not going to aid and abet him." Anyway, now that I thought about it, Kevin would be as bad as Eddie. I'm sure Enid would be insulted if she thought I as trying to set her up with my younger brother. And justifiably. In order for it to work, it had to be someone with no connection to me.

Only how could I get someone with no connection with me to do it?

"Eddie," I said, pulling the phone onto my bed, "do you know anyone who needs a date to the dance?"

"Who're you trying to fix up? Jennifer?"

"No, she's going with Alan. It's a girl in one of my classes. Enid Cortelyou."

"I didn't know you two were friends."

"We're not. I just feel sorry for her. It doesn't seem right that she's never been to a high school dance."

"I don't know. I could live without ever going to another one of them."

"We're going, Eddie. Can you think of anyone I can get to ask her? Does anyone owe you a favor?"

"Look, Kathy, I admire Enid as much as the next person, but she's not the kind of girl you invite to a dance."

"If looks are all you care about—"

"Did I say that? I'm talking about her attitude. As far as I can tell, she acts as though there's only one sex. There's just nothing appealing about her."

"It's not her fault, Eddie. She's just on the same social level we were on in the fifth grade. I didn't think I was any different than the boys then."

"Well, maybe she'll lighten up in college. Anyway, she's probably perfectly happy with the way things are."

"You don't know that. She might feel isolated and rejected for all you know."

I could hear Eddie sigh. "Well, there's Joe Morrisey," he said.

"Joe doesn't have a date?" He was a pretty cute guy not to have a date for the dance.

"He could. But the thing about Joe is, he'll do anything for money."

"You want me to *pay* him? Enid would be totally humiliated if she knew some guy was being paid to ask her out." I thought for a moment. "What would he charge?"

"It's not like he does it for a living, Kathy. I just know he's always hard up for money. I'll bet he'd do it for fifty bucks."

"That's a lot of money," I said, remembering how many hours of work it took me to save that much.

"Maybe he'd take less. You want me to sound him out?" What can I say? I've never denied that Eddie is a sweet guy.

"Would you call him right now and call me back?"

Five minutes later he called back. "Good news," he said.

"You mean he'll do it?"

"So he says. I started out at twenty-five and let him bargain me up to thirty. So, is it a deal?"

I thought of what I could do with thirty dollars. It wasn't very much, though, at the most a new sundress. I decided it was like donating the money to charity—it made me feel good and it might change Enid's life.

"It's a deal," I said. "When's he going to ask her?"

"He says he's in English with her."

"So he knows who she is?"

"Everyone knows who she is. He says he was in grade school with her and she wasn't so weird then."

"Maybe something will really come of this."

"Don't get any romantic notions, Kathy. The

only thing likely to come of it is that you keep paying Joe."

"Thanks, Eddie, I owe you one."

"One of these days, Kath, I'm going to call in all the favors you owe me."

"You know what the coach said. You don't want to get distracted from football. You're in training, kid."

"What does the coach know? He's been married twenty years."

I was wondering what to say to that but was saved by the bell, or at least by call waiting.

I used to think it was fun to talk about after we were married. We had our wedding planned, where we'd go for our honeymoon, even the names of our children. But before it seemed like a fantasy. Now, with the day fast approaching when we'd actually be able to get married, I didn't want to hear about it. I wasn't ready to be an adult. I wasn't ready to decide to settle down forever with my first-and-only serious boyfriend. I didn't even know what I wanted to do with my life.

There had to be more to life than putting Eddie through dental school, settling down, and having children.

If only I could figure out what.

9

"**H**E ASKED YOU TO JOIN THE PHYSICS CLUB?" ASKED Jennifer, looking impressed. "Wow, I wish Robert would ask me to join the drama club."

"Nothing's stopping you from joining it," I said, trying to sound as though I thought being asked was no big deal.

"Yeah, but to be personally invited. I guess the attraction's mutual, huh?"

"Don't be ridiculous, Jennifer," I said, secretly hoping she was right. "It was because I did well on the quiz. I think that was the first time he realized how much I like the class."

"That's because he doesn't have to listen to you spouting off about it all the time. You're not fooling me though, Kath. I don't doubt that you like physics, but I think it's the teacher who's the real attraction."

I grinned at her. "Well, maybe partly."

The cafeteria started to clear out as students left to attend the pep rally outside. "You want to go cheer the team?" I asked.

"Nah, let's have a second dessert, instead."

I didn't have to be asked twice. One more pep rally didn't sound all that thrilling. Now, physics, on the other hand, and Rinaldi . . .

I walked into the room where the physics club met feeling like an imposter. These were probably kids who were experimenting with atomic bombs in their basements in grade school. These were kids who won all the prizes at science fairs. These were kids who knew I was dating a football player.

All eyes turned to me as I walked through the door, and their look wasn't welcoming. The desks had been rearranged in a circle, which prevented me from sitting in the back and trying to look invisible.

I took a seat in a vacant desk and did a quick head count. There were sixteen boys, but at least there were five other girls. Three were Asian students, whom I didn't know; one was Enid, of course; and the fifth girl was small, with a funny face, and looked vaguely familiar, but I couldn't place her. Then I remembered that Kevin had dated her briefly his freshman year and after that she would call the house and ask for him about a hundred times a day and Kevin would never talk to her. I could only assume that she was smarter academically than she was about boys.

Rinaldi strolled in. He had removed his tie and suit jacket and had his sleeves rolled up, which made him look younger and even more appealing. I wondered if this was what he looked like at home, after work.

"Sorry I'm late, guys," he said, "but we had a

plumbing problem in the teachers' room and naturally it took a physicist to fix it."

Everyone laughed and he said, "Glad you decided to join us, Kathy." I was so embarrassed, especially since no one else was looking glad to see me, that when he asked for a show of hands, I realized I hadn't heard a word he had said.

"You're not coming, Kathy?" he asked me.

"I'm sorry," I said. "I didn't hear what you asked."

"It's a field trip we're taking on Saturday to Cal Tech."

I still didn't know what he was talking about and it must have shown, because he said, "You *have* heard of Cal Tech, haven't you?"

I shook my head, which made some of the boys snigger.

"The California Institute of Technology," Mr. Rinaldi explained.

"Is that a school?" I asked, and the rest of the kids broke up. I felt pretty dumb. What must Rinaldi be thinking? That I had grown up under a rock, no doubt.

Mr. Rinaldi was grinning at me. "It's where all aspiring physicists aspire to go," he said. "Let's see a show of hands of everyone who's applied there."

Every hand went up but mine.

"Well, maybe the trip would change your mind," he said to me.

"On Saturday?" I asked.

"All day," he said.

"But we have a football game on Saturday," I reminded him.

There were a few groans and a few boos at that.

"Hey, let's not put down football," said Rinaldi. "I'm a big fan myself."

Dead silence.

He shook his head in disbelief. "Don't any of you guys support your football team?"

I raised my hand.

"Well, I'm glad someone in here has some school spirit," he said, smiling at me. "But you could miss just one game, Kathy, couldn't you? You really ought to see Cal Tech."

"Her boyfriend plays on the team," said Don Shrader, the nerdiest of the nerds. I felt like killing him for letting Rinaldi know I had a boyfriend.

"Oh? What position?" asked Rinaldi.

"Wide receiver," I mumbled.

"You don't mean Eddie Lenahan?"

I nodded.

"He's great! That catch he made in the third quarter last week . . . Okay, okay, I see I'm losing most of you. So, back to the subject. The bus leaves tomorrow morning, north side of the parking lot, eight sharp. A little early for a Saturday morning, but what can I tell you."

I raised my hand.

"You don't have to raise your hand in here, Kathy."

"I'd like to go tomorrow."

"Great. Then it's all set?"

I was going to be in trouble with Eddie for missing the game and I was going to be in trouble with Jennifer for not going with her. But I wasn't about to give up the chance of spending an entire day

with Mr. Rinaldi. Plus, if Cal Tech was something
he thought I should see, then I was going to see it.
I'd worry about the consequences later.

Kevin sat as close to the door as he could get.
He stared out the window, not saying a word. I
had the feeling he was imagining bars between us
with me as his jailer.

"This wasn't my idea, you know," I said.

Silence.

"Lighten up, it's Friday."

Being grounded, though, it probably didn't make
much difference to him.

"You want me to drive by the pier? Would that
cheer you up?"

Nothing.

"Look, Kevin, don't take it so seriously. You
know Dad, he never sticks to anything. Behave
yourself for a couple of weeks and I'm sure he'll
let you go surfing again. On weekends, anyway.
He's going to get sick of you hanging around the
house all the time."

He turned to glare at me.

Okay, so a couple of weeks seem endless when
you're fifteen. It wasn't my fault; I didn't know why
he was punishing me.

I dropped him off at the house, made sure he
went inside, then drove over to Jennifer's. Her
mom let me in and I went upstairs to her room.

"I see you didn't go to the mall," I said.

"It's not any fun by myself."

"There were probably thousands of people
there."

"You know what I mean," she said.

Jennifer's room was exactly the way my mother would like mine to be. Not the decorating, that would be a little too modern and dramatic for Mom's taste, but the bed was neatly made and everything was in its place. Every time I was in it I felt like messing it up so it would look like a normal teenager lived there.

"So, you going out with Alan tonight?" I asked her.

"Yeah. How was your club?"

"I'm not too well liked in that group."

"Then why join? Except for Rinaldi's presence, of course." She smiled knowingly.

"I don't know; I guess it's a challenge. They're going on a field trip tomorrow," I said.

"You're kidding. On a Saturday? And they're not throwing you out for not going?"

"The thing is, I said I'd go."

For once in her life, Jennifer was speechless.

"Do you mind?" I asked her.

"You're not going to the game with me?"

"They're going to Cal Tech and Mr. Rinaldi thought I ought to see it."

"Cal Tech? What's Cal Tech?"

"It's a university. I guess all of them are trying to get in there."

"But you're going to UCLA."

"I'd still like to see it."

"So I'm supposed to go to the game all by myself?"

"Jen, you don't even like football. You always complain when I drag you to the games."

"That's not the point."

"Come on, Jen, it's just this once."

"We're still rooming together at UCLA next year, aren't we?"

"Give me a break, Jen, I'm only going on a field trip, okay?"

"I understand. If Robert Madrigal asked me to go on a field trip, I'd probably go." She'd probably go to the moon if Robert asked her, but that wasn't the point.

"It's not just Mr. Rinaldi." True enough. It wasn't.

"I just don't think it's very nice of you to leave me with nothing to do tomorrow."

"We'll go to the mall Sunday, okay?"

"You promise?"

"I promise."

Things were strained at my house, so after dinner I drove over to see Eddie. I was feeling pretty guilty about everything, and I wanted to see him in person.

At Eddie's house, his mom answered the door and said he was out in back, so I went out to the yard and saw Eddie and his father tossing a football back and forth.

"Catch, Kathy," said his father, throwing the football to me. "You might as well take over; my wife's dragging me to the movies."

"That means we have the house all to ourselves," said Eddie, loud enough so that his father was sure to hear.

He did. "If he gives you any trouble, Kathy, you just tell me," said Mr. Lenahan, giving me a big wink.

"I don't give her any trouble, she's the one who gives me trouble," said Eddie.

"That's the way it's supposed to be," said his father, going into the house.

"I was going to come over in a little while," Eddie said, running back to catch a pass I threw him.

"I had to get out of there."

"Kevin in trouble again?"

"Get this! He's on a hunger strike."

"Excuse me?"

"You heard me. He's now on a hunger strike to protest being grounded. Naturally that's the one thing calculated to drive my mother up the wall. She thinks she's completely failed as a parent if we don't eat everything on our plates."

"Don't let him fool you. He's probably got a stash of food in his room."

"Oh, he's not fooling me. It's just that I'm getting sick of every dinner-table conversation revolving around Kevin."

"Poor, neglected child," said Eddie, a big grin on his face.

"Eddie," I said, vaguely irritated. "It's not funny." Didn't *any*one take me seriously? What did I have to do around here? Kill someone?

Eddie quit smiling and came over to me, still holding the football. I tried to shake off my bad mood—I'd been giving him enough of a hard time lately.

Eddie put his arm around my shoulders and kissed my neck. I tried to smile.

"I didn't mean to laugh, Kath. I just think Kevin's going way overboard, that's all."

"I know he is, but I feel like I could disappear and no one would miss me."

"I would miss you," he said.

Eddie kissed my neck again.

"Hey," said Eddie. "I have some news."

"Yeah?" I could use some good news.

"Morrisey asked Cortelyou to the dance. He cornered her after English. She said no." So it wasn't good news after all.

"She said *no*?" I couldn't believe it.

"That's right. Joe said he felt stupid."

"Did he ask her nicely?"

"How would I know?"

"I can't believe she turned him down."

"Neither could Joe."

"Oh, well, it was worth a try."

"Was it worth thirty dollars?"

"What do you mean? I'm not going to pay him if he isn't going. What did it take, one minute? Does he think he's worth thirty dollars per minute?"

"You better discuss it with Joe."

"Don't worry, I will."

Eddie's mother yelled good-bye to us from the kitchen window. Eddie said, "Want to go inside and watch some TV?"

"Sure."

"In my room?"

"No, Eddie, the family room is fine."

"Yeah, I guess it is. After all, no one's home but us."

"No one's going to be home but you if you keep that up. What did you have for dessert?" I asked him.

"You didn't get dessert?"

"Nope. Kevin made his announcement and went upstairs, shortly followed by my mother and then my father. That's when I drove over here."

"Chocolate pudding with whipped cream."

"Good. And then we can have some microwave popcorn later."

"Maybe *you* ought to think about a hunger strike," he said. I kicked him.

I loved Eddie's kitchen because it was always a mess. There were dirty dishes in the sink, a greasy frying pan on the stove, and a carton of milk left out. Piles of newspapers and magazines were everywhere. Mom would die if her kitchen ever looked like that. She would be sure that some health inspector would come by and take away her license to be a housewife.

Eddie set a large bowl of chocolate pudding and a plastic container of phony whipped cream in front of me and sat down across from me at the table. He told me about how football practice had gone and what the game plan was for tomorrow. This was Eddie's idea of stimulating conversation.

Now, I love football, I always have. I find it intellectually stimulating to play and intellectually stimulating to watch. But I don't find it intellectually stimulating to talk about. And I bet that Mr. Rinaldi didn't always sit around talking football. I'm sure he could find more interesting things to talk about.

Which reminded me. It was going to be an early night because Eddie had a game tomorrow, but it was also going to be an early night because I had to be at school at eight in the morning. And I was going to have to break the news to Eddie that I would be missing his game, only I didn't know how. I had never missed watching him play since he first made a team in seventh grade.

"So you figure you're going to win tomorrow?" I asked him.

"Against Marina? Sure. Piece of cake."

"Probably be really one-sided."

"I'll be surprised if they get on the scoreboard."

I thought of saying, *Well, good, then you won't mind my missing it,* but I didn't have the guts.

"You want to go to Sandy's party tomorrow night? We could have dinner first."

"Sure," I said.

"Where do you want to go?"

"I don't care. Fatso's is fine."

"Okay, what's up? You're looking guilty, Kathy." I never had been able to fool him. Of course, I'd never needed to.

"I'm feeling guilty," I admitted.

"It doesn't seem to be affecting your appetite."

I finished the last of the pudding and pushed the bowl away. "Would you be mad at me if I missed the game tomorrow?"

"I'd kill you."

"I'm serious."

"So am I."

"Oh, come on, Eddie, what's the big deal if I miss one game?"

"I like having you there. What's so important you're going to miss a game?"

"It's a field trip."

"How come I didn't hear about it?"

I sighed. "It's the physics club. I joined the physics club."

"How come you didn't tell me?"

"I joined today. After school. You were at practice. Okay? We're going to Cal Tech."

"And this is important?"

"It's not the trip, Eddie, it's the fact that no one in that class takes me seriously. When I pointed out that there was a football game, they all looked at me as though I was crazy."

"You really care what those nerds think?"

"I care what Mr. Rinaldi thinks."

Eddie got very still.

"I really like that class, Eddie."

"So you've told me about five thousand times."

"Well I do. It's the only interesting class I have."

"More interesting than football?"

I had to think about that for a moment. "It's not more interesting than playing football, but it's more interesting than being a spectator. Anyway, it's only one game. I won't miss another."

"You better not miss homecoming. I'm up for homecoming king."

"Well, I'm not surprised. I'm sure half the team is."

"I put in your name for homecoming queen," he said, looking pleased.

"Well, take it back out, Eddie."

I could tell he thought I was kidding him. "I think we have a good chance of making it."

"Eddie, there's no way I'm going to run for homecoming queen."

"You'll win by a landslide."

"I don't want to win, Eddie. I'd feel really ridiculous being homecoming queen. Everyone would laugh at me."

"Well, your friends wouldn't laugh, and my friends wouldn't laugh. So just who is it who's going to be laughing?"

"Come on, Eddie, I hate that kind of stuff."

"Who's going to laugh, Kathy, the nerds in your physics class?"

"It's not just—"

"Who's going to laugh, this Rinaldi you're always talking about?"

"Eddie, I'm not going to put on my college application that I was homecoming queen."

"Since when did you become so serious?"

"I've always been a serious student. You don't get A's if you're not serious, you know."

"I think you better go home."

"Oh, come on, Eddie."

"I mean it. Right now I feel like strangling you, so I think you'd better leave."

"Eddie . . ."

He got up from the table and stormed out of the room. I heard the front door slam and got up to follow him, but when I got outside he was already driving away.

Great. My brother hated my guts, my best friend was mad at me, and now Eddie. For the first time in my life I was doing something for *myself*, and look where it got me.

I sure hope Mr. Rinaldi appreciated it.

10

WHEN I GOT OUTSIDE ON SATURDAY MORNING, I found I had a flat tire. It didn't take me that long to change it, but I didn't get to the school parking lot until eight on the dot. The bus was already filled and ready to go and everyone looked as though they'd been there waiting for ages.

There's a name for people like that. People who are always early, who do all their homework, who get A's in all their subjects. Since I'm one of those people, though, we won't go into that.

I boarded the bus. Mr. Rinaldi called out, "Good morning, Kathy." Everyone else ignored me.

Most of the kids were seated in pairs and I looked around for an empty seat. There was one beside Enid Cortelyou. It figured. Everyone was probably scared to sit next to her.

Well, I wasn't scared. She was human like the rest of us, wasn't she? Well, maybe not *quite* like the rest of us, but close.

As soon as I sat down, the bus took off. Enid ignored me.

It was a subdued group of people. There was no laughing or yelling or song singing, just a lot of subdued talk, most of it sounding serious.

Mr. Rinaldi got up from his seat in the front and began to walk to the back of the bus, stopping every now and then to talk to one of the kids. He looked wonderful. He was dressed exactly like me, in jeans, a sweatshirt, and running shoes. I liked seeing him in casual clothes. I pictured him in his yard, (does he have a yard?), maybe mowing the grass or something. I could take him some iced tea . . .

Most of the kids were dressed either as though they were going to lunch at Buffum's Tea Room with their grandmothers, or as though they were celebrating conformity as an art form. Rinaldi gave me a smile as he went by but didn't stop. I took a deep breath. Nice smile.

Enid continued to act as though I were invisible. If I were in her position and wanted to ignore me, I would have stared out the window at the passing scenery. Enid chose to stare straight ahead at the back of the seat in front of her.

Maybe she was thinking deep, complex thoughts. Either that or she was planning my murder.

"I could've slept another couple of hours," I said to her, watching to see if her expression would change.

It didn't. Not by so much as a flicker of her eyelid did she acknowledge that I had said anything.

I heard a chuckle from across the aisle and

looked over to see Bobby Garner grinning at me. Bobby was one of the school brains, but he was one of the cuter ones. He was also someone Eddie and I had hung out with in grade school.

"Hey, Kathy," he said.

"I didn't know you were in the physics club," I said.

"I make it for special events. So what'd you do, desert Eddie today?"

"Eddie can play football without me."

"I can remember when you threw the ball farther than him."

"I can still kick it farther," I said, which might not be true, but since Eddie never kicked it anymore, there was really no way of knowing.

"So, you applying to Cal Tech?"

"I never even heard of it until yesterday."

"Where have you been, in outer space?"

I grinned. "I can still punch you out, Bobby."

"Hey, I'm called Robert now," he said, returning my grin.

"Is that right, Bobby?"

Mr. Rinaldi, who had stopped behind us, said, "There'll be no fights on the bus, guys." This got a few derisive laughs from guys who had never punched anyone in their lives.

"Hey, Rinaldi," said Bobby. "You letting jocks in the physics club now?"

"You're talking about Kathy?" Mr. Rinaldi asked. He smiled down at me. "You're full of surprises, aren't you?" I could feel my ears start to burn.

"You know her boyfriend, Eddie Lenahan?"

Bobby said. "She broke his tooth in a fight the first time she met him. Also gave him a black eye."

Rinaldi gave me a look of mock horror.

"We were little kids at the time," I said.

"I'm glad to hear that," said Rinaldi, then continued on up the aisle. Wonderful. I'm sure he really respects my mind now, I thought.

"You have a big mouth, Garner," I said.

"Just thought you'd like someone to talk to," he said. He leaned his head over and motioned me to him. When our heads were close, he whispered, "You're wasting your time trying to talk to Cortelyou. She doesn't talk to *any*one."

"Why not?" I whispered back.

"Beats me," he said with a shrug.

I saw the boy seated next to Bobby poke him to get his attention and then whisper something to him. This was Gary Miller, who was in my physics class.

Bobby turned back to me. "Gary wants to know how you answered the last question on the quiz."

"I don't remember," I said.

"How could you not remember?"

"Probably because I didn't understand the question."

More whispering, then Bobby said, "He wants to know how you got the answer right."

"I just used my imagination. You know, like writing science fiction."

"I don't believe it," I heard Gary say. "You don't get every question right by using your imagination."

"Well, I did," I said, loud enough for him to hear.

"I study for days at a time, and she uses her imagination," Gary muttered.

I turned to see if Enid was listening to any of this, but she was still staring straight ahead, looking almost catatonic. Looking past her, I could see bumper-to-bumper traffic on the freeway.

"Rinaldi likes you," Bobby said.

"Give me a break, Bobby!" I wish, I wish.

"No, I mean it. He was telling our class about you. He said he had this new girl in his class who looked like a cheerleader but was the only one to ace the quiz." I was self-consciously pleased that he had told another class about me.

"That doesn't mean he likes me," I said casually.

"Hey, teachers always like anyone who aces a quiz. You've been in school long enough to learn that."

I was beginning to think maybe he did like me, though. The way he smiled at me, the way he had been kidding around. I saw that he was now sitting all alone up front and wished I had the guts to walk up there and sit next to him.

Which made me feel guilty. My boyfriend was playing in a football game, and instead of watching him, I was hoping to get better acquainted with Mr. Rinaldi. Which made me angry. Why should I feel like an ax murderer just because I missed *one* game in six years!

I hadn't heard a word from Eddie last night after he stormed out of his house. I was sure he'd call, but he never did. We were supposed to be going to a party tonight. I didn't think I could stand another night at home with Kevin on his hunger strike, Mom being hysterical, and Dad holding firm.

I looked at Enid again, but she was still ignoring me. I wondered what I could possibly say to get her to talk to me. It certainly wouldn't be about physics, since I didn't know enough about it yet to carry on an intelligent conversation. I wished I could ask her why she turned down Joe when he asked her to the dance, but I didn't have the guts for that, either.

Instead, I said to Bobby, "You going to the Homecoming Dance?"

"I thought I might," said Bobby, and I heard one of the other boys groan.

Our Homecoming Dance is always the weekend of Halloween, which makes it kind of fun since most of the kids wear costumes. "What're you going as?" I asked him.

"I haven't even asked anyone yet. I hear Eddie's up for homecoming king. You going to be queen?"

"Don't be ridiculous," I said, looking around to make sure no one heard him.

"What's the matter with that?" he asked me. "Hey, most of these guys would give up their grade-point average to be homecoming king."

"Oh, sure."

"And date a cheerleader."

"I'm not a cheerleader!"

"You know what I mean." And then, as though I had planned it, Bobby leaned over and said to Enid, "Hey, Cortelyou, you going to the Homecoming Dance?"

There was dead silence in the bus as everyone

strained to hear what she'd say. A couple of the guys were looking at Bobby as though he'd lost his mind. No one had ever talked to Enid like that.

Enid never even came out of her trance.

I fell in love with Cal Tech in less than an hour.

Maybe it had something to do with Mr. Rinaldi showing us around and once, taking me aside to introduce me to one of his teachers, saying, "Henry, I've got a live one here." Mostly, though, it had to do with the school itself.

We were taken to see different experiments going on, things I hadn't even dreamed of. Some of the world's best physicists talked to us, telling us what we could expect from the school. We even— and this was the high point for me—got to see a seismograph that was, at that very moment, recording an earthquake. Everything was very new, very different, and very exciting.

We had lunch in the student union and afterward visited the bookstore. I bought a book by Richard Feynman, one of their most famous physicists, and a poster of Einstein to hang on my bedroom wall. I also picked up an application. I thought that it would be interesting to see if they'd accept me. Of course I was probably going to UCLA, but it wouldn't hurt just to see.

After that we went over to the jet propulsion laboratory. This seemed to be what most of the boys liked best, but I had liked watching the earthquake being measured. I kept looking at Enid to see if I could discern any signs of excitement, but no matter what was said to us or what we saw, her expression never changed. I finally stopped watching her and hung out with Bobby instead.

I sat beside Enid again on the way home because I wanted to be alone. The rest of the group was excited and talkative; to some, I think, seeing Cal Tech had been almost a religious experience. Well, it had been something like that for me, but I wanted to savor the day in silence.

I opened Feynman's book and began to read. I was well into the third chapter when I heard a noise from beside me. I looked up and Enid was staring at me, her squinty green eyes magnified twofold behind her glasses.

Had she said something to me? Surely it would be something so intelligent that if I didn't hear it, it would be a great loss.

"Did you say something, Enid?" I whispered, our eyes locked like magnets.

"Never," I thought I heard her say, but it was said softly and surely I misunderstood.

"What?" I asked, a little louder.

"Never," she said again, this time so clearly I knew I wasn't mistaken.

Tension swept over me as she turned again to stare at the seat in front of her. Was she referring to the quiz? Something else? Could she possibly know about Joe Morrisey?

I slid down in my seat and tried to make myself as small as possible. I felt anger, like a hot wind, coming at me from her. I wanted to get up and change my seat but I was afraid to. I felt that if I moved, even as much as changing my position in the seat, she would start yelling at me, screaming horrible things.

Never? What did it mean? Was I supposed to respond to that one terse word?

I looked over again at Enid. "Never what?" I whispered, watching her expression very carefully.

She was back in her trance, in some world where she couldn't be reached. And she was freaking me out.

Something tapped my arm and I jumped.

"Sorry, did I scare you?" asked Bobby.

I looked at him and smiled with relief.

He leaned toward me and whispered, "Don't let her get to you."

"Did you hear that?" I whispered back.

"She's creepy. Just ignore her."

"She said 'never.' What do you suppose she meant?"

He grinned at me. "One time she said 'farce' to me and I mulled over it for days. I finally came to the conclusion she's just wacko."

"You think so?"

I looked back at Enid, but instead of seeing some magical person in a trance, I saw just an ordinary high school genius with no talent for getting along with people. *Never?* Give me a break! Joe Morrisey ought to be paying *me* for not having to go to the dance with her.

I got up and walked to the front of the bus and sat down beside Mr. Rinaldi. "Do you mind if I sit with you for a minute?" I asked him.

"Take as long as you want," he said, glancing

over to see what book I was holding. "Oh, Feyn-man—you're going to love that," he said.

"Was he one of your teachers?"

"No, but I heard him speak a couple of times. And when you get into physics a little more, you ought to read his lectures." I couldn't wait until I knew enough to have real conversations about it. I pictured Rinaldi and me walking along an empty road discussing the latest theories, our heads almost touching.

"I really enjoyed the field trip."

"Was it worth missing the football game?" he asked.

It had been hours since I'd thought about Eddie. "Yes. But I hope we won."

Thinking about Eddie playing football while I was so happy spending the day with Mr. Rinaldi made me uncomfortable, so I wasn't sorry when one of the guys came up to talk. I gave up my seat, but this time I took an empty seat at the back of the bus instead of sitting next to Enid. I had two thoughts: one, a book was much better company than a weirdo and two, what would it feel like to have Rinaldi's skinny body pressed against mine?

My cheeks burned and I sank lower behind my book.

DINNER WAS OVER BY THE TIME I GOT HOME, WHICH was just as well. Kevin was still on his hunger strike and Mom was in the kitchen crying over uneaten food.

"You okay?" I asked her, making myself a plate of some of the uneaten food, in this case spaghetti.

"I wish you'd take a plate up to your brother," she said, wiping her eyes with her sleeve.

"Kevin's not starving, Mom."

"You don't know that."

"I know he eats at school, and probably enough to last all day."

"You think so?"

"Yes. Will you quit worrying?"

She made a plate up for him anyway, piling enough spaghetti on it for three people.

"Did Eddie call?" I asked her.

"No, nobody called you."

"The field trip was great."

"I wish just once your brother would take that kind of interest in school."

"And I wish just once you'd take an interest in what I do in school."

"Oh, Kathy, it's just that we don't have to worry about you."

"Don't be so sure?" I could see the headlines now: Teenage girl runs off with physics teacher.

"You're doing just fine, Kathy," she said as she left the kitchen.

I felt like going after her and telling her everything wasn't fine, that some things were changing, and I wasn't sure how to handle it, but instead I reached for the phone to call Eddie. I was pretty sure he'd be over being angry with me. I wanted to do something, anything to keep me from thinking too much.

His mom answered and I asked for Eddie.

"He's not here, Kathy," said Mrs. Lenahan. "I thought he was with you."

"I just got home," I told her. "Did we win the game?"

"You weren't there?"

"I was on a field trip."

"Well, no wonder he was in a bad mood. He hardly ate anything and then was out of the house before I knew where he was going."

"Did we win?"

"Yes. Forty-five to seven."

"How long ago did he leave?"

"Oh, about an hour, I'd say."

Which meant he hadn't been on his way over here. I didn't think he'd go to the party himself, but I wouldn't put it past him to go out and drown his sorrows with his friends.

I had barely finished eating when Mom was back, grabbing my empty plate and taking it over to the sink. A dirty plate doesn't get to sit around long in our house.

"I was going to wash it," I said.

"I don't mind."

"Mom, I think I know what I want to be when I grow up," I said, wanting to lead into the subject of Cal Tech.

"You'll be a good wife and mother, darling." It was a rote answer I'd heard a hundred times.

"I don't think that's enough," I said.

"It was enough for me."

"But that's because it was what you wanted. Women are doing all kinds of things these days."

"Yes, and from the articles I've read, they're not at all happy. Wanting everything just ends up making you frustrated, Kathy."

"Jennifer's mom is an accountant."

"Yes, and she's divorced. As are most of my friends who opted for careers."

"And what about all the women without careers who end up divorced? At least if you have a career you can support yourself."

"I'd rather not think about that."

"Didn't you ever want to be anything?" I asked.

She leaned against the kitchen counter and a dreamy look came into her eyes. "I wanted to be a ballet dancer when I was a girl, but then I grew too tall."

"Oh, Mom, all little girls want to be ballet dancers. I meant something serious."

"You didn't want to be one. You wanted to be a football player. I had to bribe you to take ballet lessons, if I recall."

"I hated ballet."

"I could never understand it." She started the dishwasher, which meant I had to shout to be heard.

"Mom, I want something to look forward to."

"Aren't you going out with Eddie tonight?"

Oh, please.

"I think he's mad at me for missing the game."

"You'll make it up, Kathy. Eddie's a sweet boy."

"I'll deal with Eddie later; right now I'm worried about my future."

"Well, you don't have to worry about it now. After college is plenty of time to worry about it. If Eddie doesn't suit you, I'm sure you'll meet someone else."

"This isn't about men, Mom," I shouted, but she either didn't hear me or was ignoring me. I should have expected it, but I couldn't help feeling frustrated. What was her problem? I was amazed my parents were willing to pay for me to go to college at all, considering what a *waste* they considered it.

I got up to go to my room, but Mom handed me the plate of food. "If you're going upstairs, take this to your brother."

"He's not going to eat it."

"Please, Kathy."

I took it, but I knew Kevin wouldn't eat it. Even

when he wasn't on a hunger strike, he wasn't crazy about Mom's spaghetti.

I knocked on Kevin's door, calling out, "It's me, Kevin."

"The door's open."

I went in and found Kevin huddled on his bed. He looked hungry, but I didn't think it was for food. He had a haunted look in his eyes as though he'd lost something very precious.

"Mom sent me with this," I said, holding out the plate.

"I don't want it."

I set it down on his desk. "Do whatever you want with it."

"Kathy? What would you do if you were me?"

"I don't know." I wondered what I'd do, now, if I were forbidden to take physics. Or to see Mr. Rinaldi. I think I'd read physics anyway. I thought about Rinaldi for a minute, then decided that although I found him fascinating and attractive and different, in all honesty, I probably wouldn't kill myself if I could never see him again.

"Kathy?"

"What?"

"You've been okay. I appreciate it."

I looked at him carefully. It sounded as though he were saying good-bye.

"You're not going to do something crazy, are you?"

"Don't worry."

"If you're thinking of running away, don't do it. I'm sure Dad will lift the restrictions soon."

"I don't think I can wait."

"Look, Kevin, I don't think I have a date tonight. What if I got permission to take you to a movie?"

"Thanks, Kath, but it's not movies that I miss."

I shrugged, said, "Yell if you change your mind," and went to my own room.

I didn't really feel like going to the movies anyway. On second thought I liked the idea of having a Saturday night to myself for a change. I would hang my new poster on the wall, read the Feynman book I had started, and watch "Saturday Night Live."

I centered the poster of Einstein over his formula, and it looked wonderful. Of course I had thought Joe Montana looked wonderful up there two years ago, and last year I thought I'd never get tired of looking at Bon Jovi. But somehow Einstein was different. I could aspire to be Joe Montana when I grew up all I wanted, but it was never going to happen. Nor was being in a rock band or even meeting Bon Jovi. But I could aspire to be like Einstein. Oh, not that brilliant—I wasn't that unrealistic—but maybe I could be a physicist, even if I didn't turn out to be another Einstein.

And I suddenly knew with more certainty that I'd ever known anything, that that was what I wanted to be. A physicist. Why not? I loved it, I found it fascinating, and I knew I had it in me. I smiled at the thought of me in a white lab coat discussing important earth-shattering theories and developments.

Then my fantasies split into two scenes: me and Rinaldi, both in lab coats. Then just me in my lab coat, driving home to Eddie and our two children. The children had very white teeth.

I took out the Cal Tech application and was filling it out when my phone rang. I was sure it was Eddie and I was tempted not to answer it. I finally did on the eighth ring and it was Jennifer.

"I think you better get over here," she said.

"Hi, Jen."

"I mean it, I'm at Sandy's party," she said, but I had already figured that out by the loud music playing in the background.

"I'm not in the mood for a party tonight," I told her.

"Eddie's here."

"Alone?"

"Well, he came alone."

"Quit hinting around, Jennifer, and just tell me what's happening."

"Well, he's surrounded by groupies."

"Eddie's always surrounded by groupies. What is it, the sophomore contingent?"

"Yes, but what's different this time is that he seems to be enjoying it."

"And he probably knows you'll tell me."

"What're you doing?"

"Nothing. I just feel like staying home."

"On a Saturday night?"

"It was a long day, Jen. I just feel like getting in bed and watching some TV."

"All right, but don't say I didn't warn you. I'll keep an eye on him so he doesn't get carried away."

"Don't tell him you called."

"Don't worry."

I was feeling slightly annoyed over Eddie and the sophomores. He was probably doing it just to get to me. Fine. He got to me, a little. Even though confused about my feelings for Eddie these days, I was pretty sure that he hadn't changed his feelings for me. I knew that I still cared for him. I would always love him, no matter what happened.

But in reality I wondered what I'd do if Mom knocked on my door and told me Mr. Rinaldi was downstairs to see me. Not that it would happen, particularly not while I was still in high school. But in nine months it would be perfectly okay. And he did seem to like me, I wasn't mistaken about that.

I was probably being ridiculous. It wasn't the first time I'd had a crush on a teacher. It was just the first time that the age difference hadn't been great. And the teacher had been so cute. And I had been confused about Eddie. For all I knew, Rinaldi might have a secret crush on Enid Cortelyou. But I knew deep down he liked me better than Enid.

I finished filling out the application, put it in an envelope, then went downstairs to get a stamp.

Dad was in the den, working at his desk. "Could I talk to you for a minute?" I asked him.

"If it's about Kevin, I don't want to hear it."

"It's about me."

He turned around and smiled at me. "Sure, honey, what is it?"

"I saw Cal Tech today."

"I know you did. Did you have a good time?"

"I loved it, Dad."

"Well, good, honey. Not going out with Eddie tonight?"

"I'm staying home. I wanted to talk to you about Cal Tech, Dad."

"I'm listening."

"I'd like to go there."

Dad started to chuckle.

"I'm serious," I said, annoyed at his chuckle. If it was Kevin or Mike expressing an interest in Cal Tech, he certainly wouldn't be chuckling.

"Why Cal Tech? They don't even have a football team." He was smiling at me. In fact, he was humoring me, and I began to lose any sense of humor I might have had.

"I don't go out for football, in case you hadn't noticed," I said.

Dad seemed oblivious to the sarcasm. "What about Eddie?"

"I'm not talking about Eddie, I'm talking about me. I really like physics, Dad, and that's the school to go to."

"Honey, I doubt whether they'd even accept you. Every brain in the country applies there."

"You might be surprised to hear, Dad, that some of my teachers consider me a brain."

"You're a bright girl, Kathy, I'd be the first to admit it. But we're talking about stiff competition here."

"But if they did accept me? Could I go?"

"I'm sorry, Kath, but financially it's just not possible. The expenses for Mike's medical school are going to be astronomical. You'll be in college at the same time, and then Kevin two years later."

"Why are you willing to pay for an expensive school for Mike but not for me? And Kevin doesn't even want to go to college."

"He's going, believe me."

"I know that I want to be a physicist, Dad. I was hoping you would support my decision. Or at least not ridicule it."

Dad's lips tightened.

"Leave the science to Mike, honey."

"But *I'm* good at it."

"Maybe you could be a lab technician, something like that. I guess it wouldn't hurt for you to have a skill in case you ever have to support yourself, God forbid."

"Dad! This isn't the Dark Ages! Maybe I *want* to support myself!"

"You and Eddie having problems?"

"Eddie has nothing to do with this!" I was practically screaming, but Dad seemed impervious.

"A dental technician wouldn't be a bad idea. Then you could help him out occasionally."

I couldn't believe my ears. I wanted to be a *physicist* and he actually thought I'd be satisfied being a lab technician. I decided I had to go kill something. I don't even think he noticed when I left the room.

I stalked down to the corner and mailed my application. But if Dad wouldn't pay for it, it didn't matter whether they accepted me or not. I didn't think I could possibly get a scholarship. People like Enid got scholarships. I'd never even entered anything in a science fair. I'd have to find someway. . . .

* * *

"Saturday Night Live" was a repeat and I turned it off around midnight. A few minutes later I heard Mom and Dad come up to bed and I snarled in their general direction. I hadn't heard any noise from Kevin's room and I wondered if he was in there waiting for everyone to go to sleep before he ran away.

I started to fantasize about what it would be like to be married to Mr. Rinaldi. I wondered if we would talk about physics in bed.

I heard a car pull up outside and stop. I thought, *Oh, no, Kevin's got some friend who's going to help him run away.* I got up and looked out the window. It was Eddie's car. If he started honking, my father would have a fit.

I put on some shorts and a T-shirt and ran downstairs barefoot. When I opened the front door, he was still out there, and when I got close to his car, I could see him slumped at the wheel.

I opened the door and slid inside. "What're you doing here?" I asked him. After my fight with Dad, I was actually glad to see Eddie. I needed an ally.

"You mad at me, Kath?"

"I thought you were mad at me."

"I was. We won the game."

"I know, your mom told me."

"You called me?"

"As soon as I got home."

He put his arm around me. It felt good having someone on my side and I moved over close to him. Lately I had been forgetting that he was supposed to be my best friend as well as my boyfriend. Things had always seemed better before when I could talk them over with Eddie.

"I went to the party," he said.

"Did you have fun?" I asked, not even annoyed about the groupies anymore. It wouldn't have been Eddie's doing, anyway.

"You're not mad?"

"No. I'm sorry I missed the game."

"How was the trip?"

"It was okay," I said, feeling guilty about having liked it so much, and about making solitary plans for my future.

"Listen, you want to go to Fatso's and get a burger?"

That was about the best offer I'd had all night.

"I'd love to, but I don't have any shoes on."

"I'll go in and get the burgers."

He started the car and was just pulling off, when I looked back to see if my parents' light had gone on and saw Kevin coming around the side of the house.

"Stop," I said to Eddie.

"What's the matter?" he said, slamming on the brakes.

"Kevin's sneaking out. I think he's running away."

Eddie backed up and I opened the window and called softly to Kevin.

He walked over to my window and looked in. "Don't worry, I'm not running away," he said.

"Where are you going?"

"I just wanted to walk down to the beach, that's all. I'm going stir-crazy in there."

"We're going to Fatso's," I said, "you want to come?"

"Come on, I'll buy you a burger," said Eddie.

"You don't mind?" Kevin asked him.

"Go on, get in the back," said Eddie. "We'll even go down to the beach afterward." I had a warm feeling inside. Eddie was a sweet guy.

Kevin climbed into the car looking happier than I'd seen him look in days.

"I hear you're on a hunger strike," said Eddie.

"Yeah, what a joke," muttered Kevin. "It lasted for real about six hours."

"Can't you and your dad come to some kind of compromise?" Eddie asked.

"You know my dad. Kathy could probably cut classes and go surfing every day and he'd think it was amusing, but boys are supposed to be serious students."

"I didn't know you knew that," I said.

"What, are you kidding? He hardly even glances at your report cards. Mine he memorizes."

"I guess you should've been the girl," I said.

"I don't want to be a girl," said Kevin. "Girls aren't good surfers."

"A sexist remark if I ever heard one," I said.

"Personally, I'm glad Kathy's the girl," said Eddie, reaching over and taking my hand.

"You should be," I said. "If I were a boy, I'd probably have your position on the team and you'd be out of luck."

"I heard you talking to Dad tonight," said Kevin. "Was it about me?"

"No."

"Oh," said Kevin, losing interest.

"Was it about me?" asked Eddie.

"Boy, you two sure have big egos," I said, changing the subject to the football game before he asked any more questions.

We loaded up with food at Fatso's and drove down to the beach. We sat on the pier to eat and I thought Kevin would be devouring the food like a starving person, but it was the sight and sound of the ocean he was devouring.

We left Kevin to watch the waves and took a walk down the beach. It was cold out and Eddie gave me his jacket. We stopped a couple of times and kissed. It seemed like ages since we had been together.

"Jennifer's mad at me for not going to the game with her," I said.

"So am I."

"Everyone's mad at me. You. Jennifer. Even Enid Cortelyou."

Eddie laughed. "Enid's mad at you?"

"She's so weird, Eddie," I said, and told him about her behavior on the bus.

"Sounds like a fun day," he said.

"At least Bobby Garner was along. I hadn't talked to him in years."

"Bobby's okay."

"He told Mr. Rinaldi how I had broken your tooth."

"Rinaldi knows you're going with me?"

"He knew already. He thinks you're a great player."

"What does he think of you?"

"Come on, Eddie, he's my teacher."

"Yeah, and he looks like a college student. Anyway, teachers have been known to be interested in students."

"I can't believe you're jealous of Mr. Rinaldi." Actually I guess I could.

"You're acting different lately."

"Just because I missed one football game—"

"It's not just that," he said, stopping and putting his arms around me.

"If it's because I don't want to be nominated for homecoming queen, Eddie, that's not being different. I've always thought that stuff was stupid."

"Okay, okay, it was just a dumb idea I had."

"We better get back," I said, "before my parents wake up and find me and Kevin missing."

When we got back, all the lights were on in the house and my older brother's car was in the driveway.

"Now I'm in for it," said Kevin.

12

EDDIE CUT THE ENGINE. "YOU WANT ME TO COME IN with you?" he asked me.

"No, it's okay." I turned around in the seat to talk to Kevin. "Go in the back way while I create a diversion in the front. They might not even know you're not home."

Kevin got out of the car and slipped into the darkness at the side of the house and I kissed Eddie good night.

I made a lot of noise going in the front door, but neither Mom nor Dad appeared. Which wasn't surprising since I heard them going hot and heavy with Mike in the kitchen. I couldn't imagine what he'd done to get them so upset unless he got thrown out of school, but that wasn't like Mike.

I peeked into the kitchen and saw Mom in her robe, a turban over her head covering her hair, which she set every night of her life. Dad, dressed only in cutoff jeans, was red in the face and looked close to a heart attack. Mike was sitting at the table having a cup of coffee.

"Hi, Mike," I said, stepping into the room.

"How's it going, Kathy?"

"Okay," I said, admiring his new, bushy mustache. Mike is the best-looking one in the family. His dark hair is curly and his eyes are practically black. He also has a great body from all the weights he lifts.

"Kathy, we're having a private discussion in here," said my father.

"It sounded like a fight to me," I countered.

"Kathy," warned my father.

"You want to know what's happening?" said Mike. "I'm dropping premed, that's what's happening. I want to major in art, but of course the arts aren't accepted in this house. No one in this house would know a cubist from a Postimpressionist."

I wasn't surprised. As a matter of fact, I don't know why I had never thought of it before. Mike had been drawing pictures for as long as I could remember. "I think that's wonderful," I told him, knowing instinctively that it was exactly right for him. His talent would be wasted in medical school.

"No one asked for your opinion," said my father, but he was diverted by the appearance of Kevin, now wearing pajamas and simulating a yawn.

"Hey, Mike," he said, sounding sleepy.

"This doesn't happen to be a family reunion," said my father.

"I'll just make us all some scrambled eggs," said Mom, who always felt more in control when she was at the stove.

"I've got one son who wants to drop out of high

school and be a surfer, and another who wants to drop out of premed and be an artist. What did I do wrong? I would've given anything to be able to go to med school," said Dad, the pharmaceutical salesman.

"And apparently no daughter at all," I snapped. Dad didn't respond.

"It's not too late, Dad," said Mike. "Lots of guys your age are going back to school."

"And just who do you think will support the family?"

There was dead silence for a moment except for the sound of Mom breaking eggs.

"Well, if Mike's not going to med school, can I go to Cal Tech?" I asked my father. Might as well make some use of the situation.

"You stay out of it," said Dad.

"Cal Tech?" asked Mike. "What's this all about?"

"I want to be a physicist," I told him.

"Go help your mother," said Dad. I rolled my eyes.

My mother turned and smiled at Mike. "But darling, you always got such good grades in science."

"That's because of my drawings," said Mike. "I always drew the best insects, the best frog parts, and the best nervous systems. It was the only thing I ever liked about science, getting to do the drawings."

"Anyone for a scrambled-egg sandwich?" asked Mom.

"No thanks," I said. "I'm not hungry." Cheap shot, Kathy.

"Kevin?" she asked, looking at him hopefully.

"I'm still on a hunger strike," said Kevin, looking every inch the martyr.

There was no point in staying. I was leaving the kitchen when Mike said, "You going to be up for a while, Kath? I'd like to talk to you."

"Sure," I told him, "just knock on my door."

As soon as I left the kitchen, I could hear Dad starting up again.

Mike was looking at my poster of Einstein. "You're really into this, huh?" he asked.

"I love it," I said. "I never knew anything could be so interesting."

"It's heavy stuff, Kath."

"It's fascinating. Didn't you like physics?"

"Like it? Sorry, but I fail to see the fascination. That doesn't mean I don't think it's great for you, though."

"Mom and Dad think I'm nuts."

He sat down on the edge of my bed. "Well, that makes it unanimous. They think we're all nuts."

"You're really dropping premed?"

"Sure I am. Why should I do something just because Dad wanted to do it? He's got to live his life, I've got to live mine."

"Kevin wants to be a surfer."

"Well, Kevin's got to learn to lighten up. Surfing's a hobby, not a profession. I think I've got Dad talked into lifting the restriction at the end of the week, though. I told him if he didn't, Kevin was sure to run away."

"He's already thinking about it."

"I'll talk to him in the morning."

"I sent in an application to Cal Tech," I said.

"Don't get your hopes up."

"Thanks a lot!" My God, not Mike, too?

"Sorry, Kathy, I'm just trying to be realistic."

"I happen to get straight A's, Mike, in case you hadn't noticed, which wouldn't be surprising in this family."

"Hey, I'm on your side. It's just that there will be a lot of kids applying, all of them with straight A's."

"Oh, well, I guess it doesn't matter. Dad won't let me go there anyway. He says he can't afford it with your medical school."

"It's not just that. He doesn't think investing in a girl is a good investment."

"I can't believe he still thinks like that. Women can be astronauts, Supreme Court justices, and prime ministers. We're not all Mrs. Cleaver, you know."

"I know, Kath—sometimes I wonder where Mom and Dad have been the last twenty years. So what does Eddie think about it?"

"I haven't asked his permission yet," I said icily. "Actually, I haven't told him. We're supposed to be going to UCLA together."

"Do what you have to do, Kathy, and don't let the folks slow you down."

"That's it? That's all the advice I'm going to get from my wise older brother?"

"That's it, kid. Any advice for me?"

"No, but I think you'll be a wonderful artist."

"I'll be a happy one, anyway."

We were sitting in the pizza place at the mall having lunch and Jennifer was looking decidedly guilty. I wondered what *she* had to look guilty about. I was the one who had applied to Cal Tech without telling her.

"Steve was at the party last night," she finally said. Then she bit into her second slice and acted as though she hadn't said anything.

"So?"

"So what?"

"So why are you telling me Steve was at the party?"

"I don't know; I just thought I'd mention it."

Jennifer never just *mentioned* things. "Was he with Marcy?" I asked.

She started to smile. "No."

"Someone else?"

Her smile got wider. "No."

"So maybe he's not seeing her anymore."

"He says he hasn't seen her since Mandy's party."

"You mean you talked to him?"

"I could hardly avoid it, Kathy, the party wasn't all that big."

"So what are you trying to tell me, Jen?"

"He was coming on to me. It was obvious to everyone. Some people came up and asked me if we were back together again. Of course not when Alan was around."

"So what does it mean? You getting back together?"

"Would you think I was crazy?"

"Why should I think you're crazy? I think you still love him."

"The thing is, he'd put a lot of pressure on me

again. But you know, Kath, I'm thinking what difference does it really make? What am I going for, a prize or something? I might as well just do it and get it over with."

"That's a cheerful thought, but it's your decision, Jen."

"It's the only thing we ever argued about. I'll be eighteen in three months. I mean, what am I waiting for?"

"You sound like you're trying to convince yourself."

"Well, I keep thinking . . . What if it turns out to be no big deal?"

"I know," I said, having had the same thought about a million times.

"Of course if it isn't any big deal, then why not?"

"Jen, you know what I think the big deal about it is?" She was looking at me wide-eyed as though I were about to impart some wisdom. "It's like reading books and always having to stop at the last chapter."

"I always read the last chapter first," said Jennifer.

"You know what I mean. It's like having to walk out of a movie before the final scene. We do everything else and then stop right before we finish. I know Eddie's frustrated, and it frustrates me, too, when I let it. You just get left up in the air, you know?"

Jennifer nodded. "I know. So what's stopping *you*?"

"I don't know. I think it's because I'm afraid I'll be disappointed. Maybe I'm just chicken."

"I admit I'm chicken," said Jennifer.

"Lately, though, I've been thinking it might be something else. Eddie's got our whole future planned out, and I'm afraid if I did it, I would be making some kind of commitment." There. It was out. I had said it.

"You'd feel you had to marry him?"

"I know that sounds stupid. I know you don't have to marry someone just because you've had sex."

"I thought you wanted to marry him."

"Maybe I do, but I don't want to feel I *have* to. And with him, I think if I did it I'd feel locked in."

"Would you do it with Rinaldi?"

"Jennifer!"

"Don't look so shocked."

"If I won't do it with Eddie, why would I do it with him?"

"I sometimes wish Robert Madrigal would sweep me off my feet and ravish me."

"*Ravish* you?"

"It means—"!

"I know what it means. What you mean is that you want the decision taken out of your hands."

"I guess so."

"I'm sure Steve would oblige."

"I don't think Steve has all that much experience. What if he's a lousy lover?"

"You're hardly in a position to know the difference."

She grinned. "You're right."

"Let's change the subject. It's making me nervous."

I ordered a pizza to go to take home to Kevin.
He's the only person I know who prefers cold pizza
to hot. Then we made the round of the stores, Jennifer trying on practically everything she saw in
black.

In one store she tried on a slinky black dress
and modeled it for me. It was amazing how much
older she looked in it. "If you wore that to a bar,
they probably wouldn't ask for ID," I said.

Jennifer admired herself in the mirror. "Well,
we're almost eighteen, you know. I don't think
we're going to look all that different at twenty-
one."

Looking at her in that dress, I could believe Robert Madrigal could be interested in her. I wondered
if I looked that old, but when I stood next to her
in front of the mirror in my shorts and T-shirt, all
I saw was a high school girl.

"You look older than I do," I complained.

"Well, yeah, in that outfit you're wearing. Why
don't you try this on?"

"I look terrible in black."

"Don't be ridiculous—you'd look great in black."

I hated dresses, and I didn't like black, but I followed her back to the dressing room and gave it
a try.

"You look good," Jennifer said. "A little makeup
and no one would believe you weren't in college."

It was strange seeing myself the way I had pictured myself looking when I grew up. Maybe this
was it. Maybe I was already grown up, but still
stuck in high school because of age requirements.

Maybe Mr. Rinaldi saw me as a woman.

"Take it off, I saw it first," said Jennifer. "I'm going to put it on layaway and beg my mother to buy it for me."

I wouldn't have to beg. My mother was always trying to get me to wear a dress.

On the way out of the mall we stopped in the store I used to work in so I could say hi to the pals I had made during the summer.

Myra, the assistant manager, came over and gave me a hug. "Kathy, it's good to see you. When are you going to come back to work?"

"I'm pretty busy at school," I told her.

"We have lots of students working here. I could sure use you a couple of nights and weekends."

I saw Jennifer making a face behind her back. She knew how relieved I had been to see the last of the place.

"Her boyfriend is on the football team," Jennifer said to Myra. "He'd kill her if she didn't come to the games."

"We could work around that," said Myra.

I thought of the money I could make, the money I might need if, by some fluke, I got accepted at Cal Tech. I remembered what Mike had said about doing what I had to do. Well, making money for college might be what I had to do, and this store was as good a place as any. In fact, it was probably better than most.

"Okay," I said to Myra. "As long as you let me switch hours with someone if I have a big test coming up."

"And don't forget your discount," Myra said, obviously not impressed with the outfit I was wearing.

"I can't believe you did that," Jennifer said as soon as we were out of the store.

"I'd like to make some money."

"But you've got to drive Kevin home after school."

I had forgotten all about that. "My mother will have to pick him up. It won't kill her to miss a garden-club meeting."

Jennifer smiled, but complained, "I hardly see you anymore as it is."

"Jennifer, the way you like clothes, I'm surprised you aren't working here. If you did, you wouldn't have to always be begging your mother."

"You think they'd hire me?"

"Sure. You know a lot more about clothes than I do."

"It's not like I have a heavy schedule."

"It'd be fun. Maybe we could get the same hours."

"But I want to try out for the play, and that would mean rehearsals every day after school."

I gave up arguing with her. I couldn't expect her to be motivated to make money just because I was. But I felt good about my decision. Maybe if I showed Dad how serious I was, how I was willing to work and pay for some of my expenses, he might be willing to pay for the rest. And if he wouldn't, I'd just find some other way.

13

THINGS SEEMED DIFFERENT WHEN I WALKED INTO physics class on Monday. For one thing, most of the kids smiled at me. It seemed I was starting to be accepted. I think it had more to do with the field trip than the quiz results, but whatever the reason, I was relieved.

I took my seat at the back and was opening up the text when Mr. Rinaldi came into the room. I saw him look around the class and then do a double take, and I followed his eyes to where Enid Cortelyou was sitting. Or at least I thought it was Enid.

Something had happened to her and the transformation was startling. Previously limp hair that had been worn so that it mostly obscured her face, was now frizzed and standing out from her head in the manner of Einstein. Bushy eyebrows that had made one straight line across her face had been thinned and separated. Her face suddenly took on bone structure. She still wasn't wearing

123

any makeup, which would have further improved her looks, but it was a definite change for the better.

Nobody seemed to notice the difference except me and Mr. Rinaldi. No one was appraising her or even darting furtive glances in her direction. It was a remarkable change, though, and I wondered what had brought it on.

Then I noticed her clothes. Instead of the polyester outfits she usually wore, the ones that looked as though they had been handed down by some great aunt, she was wearing a long cotton skirt with a black T-shirt. Black boots took the place of her usual flats. If I didn't know better, I would think she'd gone out for the drama club.

I was openly staring at her, unable to get over the evolution from brainy-and-boring to eccentric-but-interesting, when she turned around and saw me staring. I thought, *Oh-oh, now comes the hateful glare again*, and nearly fell out of my desk when she smiled at me. A fleeting smile, but a smile nonetheless. I smiled back and could have sworn she blushed before turning back around in her seat.

Mr. Rinaldi started telling us about Schrödinger's cat. And right in the middle of listening to this, for no reason at all, my mind flashed *Mr. Rinaldi*. Was Enid's new mode of dress an effort to attract his attention? Was she now openly competing with me for his attention? And, most importantly, did I care?

Well, maybe. Right now, with her improved appearance, they wouldn't make an unlikely looking couple.

Schrödinger's cat turned out to be far less interesting than what was actually going on in class.

* * *

I kept looking up, watching for Enid Cortelyou to go through the cafeteria line. I wasn't paying much attention to what Jennifer was saying. It was about Steve, and I'd heard it all before.

"Who are you looking for?" she finally asked.

"I'll let you know when I see her," I said.

"Oh." At the word *her*, she quickly lost interest.

About a minute later I saw Enid heading down one of the aisles in our direction. "Look," I said to Jennifer, trying not to be obvious when I nodded in Enid's direction.

"That's not Enid Cortelyou, is it?"

"Can you believe it?"

Jennifer was outright staring, and I said, "Jen, don't be so rude."

"Well, I can't believe it, that's all."

Even Enid's posture was better. She was still a little hunched over, but nothing like she usually was. As she passed by our table, I said, "Hi, Enid," trying to make it sound casual.

Enid looked at me and her mouth formed a word, but no sound came out. Then she was past our table and headed for the corner where she hid out to eat her lunch.

"Weird," said Jennifer, her eyes following Enid.

"I think she looks a lot better."

"She does. It's just a shock, that's all. I guess I'm used to seeing her looking like someone's mother."

I saw Jennifer look up and I turned and saw the sophomore girl from the physics club standing by the table.

"Hi," I said.

"I hate to be a fink, but I thought you ought to know something," she said.

I immediately jumped to the conclusion that she had also noticed Enid. "That's okay, feel free to be a fink," I said, smiling at her.

"It's Kevin."

"Kevin?"

"Yeah, he's not in school. He told me about you being responsible for him, and I thought you ought to know."

"Do you know when he left?"

"All I know is he wasn't here second period. Don't tell him I told you, okay?"

I nodded at her, then looked over at Jen. "I've got to go after him."

"You'll miss next period."

"So what are they going to do to me? I haven't cut a class in ages. I can't believe he did this. Dad was going to let him off the end of the week."

"I guess the surf's up."

"I'll see you later, Jen. I'm going to see if Eddie will go with me."

Eddie sat at the other end of the cafeteria with the rest of the jocks. I hated going over there because the guys always made a big production of girls who approached their table. I ignored all their teasing, though, and went straight to Eddie.

"I just found out Kevin's not in school," I said to him. "Can you go down to the pier with me?"

"Sure," he said, getting right up and following me out to the parking lot. Not a word about our possibly getting in trouble. When I needed him, Eddie was always there for me.

We took his car, and as soon as we were out of the parking lot, I said, "Maybe we should just go back. It's not like he's going to listen to me."

"He'll listen to me," said Eddie. "I'll drag him back by force if I have to. This is really stupid of him."

"I don't think he can help it. He's really obsessed with surfing. It's as important to him as breathing."

"Let's not get carried away, Kath. What he is, is bored with school, that's all. I'd rather be at the beach every day, too. Who wouldn't?"

I was worried about Kevin, but being with Eddie was comforting. I thought fleetingly about what a good father he would be. Would I have asked Rinaldi to help me look for Kevin? No way.

Eddie and I got there in less than ten minutes but took another five to find a parking spot. There were an awful lot of cars parked along Pacific Coast Highway for a weekday, and even some fancy looking trailers. There were also more people at the beach than the weather warranted.

"Something's happening down there," said Eddie, who, being taller, had a better view of the beach.

"The cops aren't down there, are they?"

"It looks as though they're filming something."

We were close enough for me to see, now, and I could see part of the beach cordoned off. I also saw the cameras. Filming movies and TV shows wasn't an unusual sight where we lived, being so close to L.A., but I didn't know why Kevin would be there. He wasn't one of those people who would go out of their way to see something like that.

There are a lot of people who do, though, and

most of them seemed to be on the beach. Out on the water I could see surfing going on.

"Do you see Kevin?" I asked Eddie.

"They all look alike from here."

"I don't know what to do. They're obviously not going to let us go through to look for him."

Eddie reached down and started to untie his shoes.

"What are you doing?" I asked him.

"Hey, it's beautiful out, we're not in school, so we might as well enjoy ourselves."

I pulled mine off, too, and we walked down onto the sand and tried to get close enough to see what was being filmed. There were quite a few kids down there for a school day, and I saw Jordan, one of Kevin's friends.

"What're they filming?" I asked him.

"A rock video."

"Where's the music?" asked Eddie, loud enough for one of the camera men to hear and give him a scornful look.

"Have you seen Kevin?" I asked Jordan.

"That's him, right there," he said, pointing to a lone figure coming in on a wave.

"Isn't he in their way?"

"I think they're using him," said Jordan.

"For what?"

"In the video. He and two other guys. I didn't get picked."

"Did you know about this before today?" I asked him.

"Nah. They just showed up about ten this morning."

"There's nothing we can do, Kathy," said Eddie. "He's fifteen, you're not his mother, and he probably figures this is worth getting in trouble for."

"I guess," I said.

"You want to stop by Fatso's? You didn't give me a chance to finish my lunch."

"Why not," I said. "I'm only missing chorus anyway. Parker probably won't even notice I'm not there." When she took roll call, some kids answered *here* for about five different people and she never knew the difference. I figured Jennifer would do it for me.

When we got to Fatso's, I was feeling that secret thrill you get when you know you're supposed to be in school instead of enjoying yourself, and I was a little jealous that Kevin got to feel that all the time.

I ordered, too, since I didn't enjoy cafeteria food all that much, and then I remembered about Enid. I told Eddie about it and he thought it was funny.

I said, "I just had an idea, Eddie. If she's out to change herself, maybe Joe should try asking her to the dance again."

"You're determined to get your money's worth, aren't you?"

"I told you, I'm not paying him if he's not going. Do you think he'd be willing to try again?"

"After she said no? She didn't even thank him. Just said no and walked off."

"Well, maybe she'll say yes the next time."

"I'll ask."

"So what was going on at your house Saturday night? What was Mike doing home?"

"You're not going to believe this, Eddie, but

Mike's decided he'd rather be an artist than a doctor."

Eddie started to grin. "I bet your dad had a heart attack."

"Just about."

"I know mine would. He's got his heart set on my being a dentist."

"That's different; you want to be a dentist."

"A dentist's not something you *want* to be, Kath. It's a good, steady profession, but it's not something you can get excited about."

"You never told me you didn't want to be a dentist," I said. He shrugged. "Why complain?" Come to think about it, he had never talked about being a dentist. About the only thing I ever saw him getting excited about was football. Well, maybe one other thing.

"Do you remember learning about Schrödinger's cat?" I asked him.

Eddie choked on his Coke. "You're not going to start with that again, are you?"

"I just wondered."

"You think *I* have a one-track mind. All I hear from you anymore is physics. Why didn't you take it last year when I was taking it? We could've studied together."

I wanted to tell him about applying to Cal Tech, but I knew he'd think I was betraying him, and in a way he was right. Instead I said, "I'm going to get my job back at the mall, I think."

"Yeah?"

"I figure I might as well. I don't have anything

better to do after school, and I wouldn't mind making some money."

"I wouldn't mind getting a job after football season."

"They hire guys there."

"I'm not working in a clothing store."

"It's that or fast food."

"I have nothing against fast food. We're sitting here eating it, aren't we?"

"Speaking of which, I can't wait for dinner tonight. If Kevin doesn't drive my father over the edge with this, I don't know what will."

"Hey, Kath," said Eddie, and I saw the gleam in his eyes. "You want to play hooky the rest of the day and go over to my house? No one's home."

I groaned and put my head down on the table. Eddie laughed. I have to admit, for one brief millisecond, I almost considered it.

Kevin was stuffing himself with food as though his hunger strike had been for real. My father was ignoring it and even my mother wasn't urging him to eat this time. Stuffed from two lunches, I just sat and watched the proceedings.

"I knew you had nerve, Kevin," said my father, and I could tell it took an effort for him to keep his voice under control, "but this . . . *this* kind of nerve can only be called colossal." He paused and looked around the table for confirmation. My mother was looking down at her plate.

Kevin had asked my father to sign a release for the production company making the video so that he could miss school again tomorrow.

"They're paying me, Dad," Kevin mumbled.

"What?"

"I said they're paying me."

"You're going to school, Kevin, if I have to take you there myself and sit with you in your classrooms." Dad's voice was a little bit louder this time.

Looking put upon, Kevin said, "We're getting paid two hundred dollars a day."

Dad opened his mouth and shut it again.

"Two hundred?" said my mother, clearly impressed.

I was pretty impressed, too. I wouldn't make that in a week at the mall.

"It's work, Dad," said Kevin, using his most beguiling tone. "Hard work, too."

"I'm sure the school would excuse him for this," I said, not sure at all but earning a grateful look from Kevin.

"I suppose we could call and find out," said Mom.

"Am I completely in the wrong here?" asked Dad, his words coming out like thunder. "Am I a rotten father? Is that it? Should I sign permission for my son to ditch school again?"

"It's good life experience, Dad," said Kevin. "I might want to go into video when I get out of school."

"I thought you were dropping out," my father reminded him.

"I don't know," said Kevin, "this looks pretty interesting. I was talking to the director and he said it was a good field to get into." As a con artist, Kevin deserved an A+.

"Well, if it gets him interested in getting an education," said my mother, but Dad ignored her.

"Do you think we could have a few rules around here?" asked Dad.

"Sure," said Kevin.

"Like going to school when you're supposed to."

"Sure," said Kevin.

"And not ditching when the surf's up."

"Do you think I could have a video camera for Christmas?" asked Kevin, and I really admired his nerve.

"You didn't answer my question," said Dad.

"If you let me do this, I promise I won't ditch anymore this year."

"This *school* year," Dad said.

"Right," said Kevin, "that's what I meant."

"I don't believe I'm doing this," said my father shaking his head.

"It's nice that Kevin's found a new interest," said Mom, and I knew she'd be out shopping for a video camera for Kevin. I tried to think of what I wanted for Christmas so I could also get my order in early, but nothing came to mind.

"All right, Kevin," said my father, signing the release form and handing it across the table to Kevin. "Now what I'd like you to do, as a token of your good faith, is go upstairs now and do your homework."

"I'll try, Dad," said Kevin, "but I've got an early shoot in the morning."

Kevin, the video star, didn't know when to let well enough alone.

14

I WAS GETTING MY CALCULUS BOOK OUT OF MY locker on Wednesday when someone came up behind me and grabbed me in a bear hug.

"Not here, Eddie," I said, turning around so that I was in his arms.

He gave me a quick kiss on the nose. "Let's get in your locker and do it."

I started to laugh.

"Well, okay, so I wouldn't fit. It's the thought that counts, right?"

He started to push me back into my locker and some of the boys standing around started to yell out things like, "Way to go, Lenahan," and "Score one for the school!"

"You're ruining my reputation," I told him, but I was still laughing.

"I'm trying to," he said, "but you just won't let me."

"Good try."

He stood back with a pleased smile on his face,

and I thought it was about what he had just done. But then he said, "I've got a surprise for you."

"For me? What?"

"Let's hear you beg."

"Eddie, I'm going to be late for calculus."

"Then you better start begging fast."

"Please," I said, humoring him.

"Enid's going to the dance."

"Are you serious? Joe asked her again?"

"Yes, absolutely, and no, he didn't. He wouldn't."

"Let me get this straight. Joe *didn't* ask Enid, and Enid *is* going to the dance."

"That's right."

"With *who*?" I screamed. I pushed him against the lockers and tried to tickle the information out of him. Eddie couldn't stop laughing.

"I'll tell you! Please!"

I stood in front of him, hands on hips, glaring at him. Eddie caught his breath.

"She's going with a guy from your physics class," he said. "Gary Miller."

Gary Miller. I tried to place him. It came to me. He was the guy sitting next to Bobby Garner on the field trip. The one who had not believed that I had done well on the quiz. Eddie grinned at me.

"You happy?"

"Well, yeah." I *was* happy that Enid was going to the dance, but I couldn't understand why anyone would pick Gary Miller over Joe Morrisey. Oh well. To each his own.

Mr. Rinaldi gave me a big smile when I walked into physics. He was wearing a white shirt and a weird navy blue tie with little rocket ships all over it. I knew I wasn't fooling myself, he really did like me. But I'd been the teacher's pet before, and I also wasn't fooling myself that it was any more than that. I might be hoping, but I really wasn't fooling myself.

I quickly looked over to see if Enid had noticed, but for once I had beaten her to class.

When she did come in, I saw she was looking even more changed. She saw me looking at her and smiled. A real smile this time, and it made her look almost pretty. She had some lipstick on, but it was the wrong color for her complexion.

"Project time, guys," said Mr. Rinaldi, getting everyone's attention. "I want you all to pick a particular area of study you're interested in and do a little investigating. This can consist of anything from experiments to deep—and I mean *deep* thinking. Write up a little proposal so that I can okay it before you begin. Any questions?"

Of course there were questions. You gather all the school brains into one classroom, and all you get are questions.

I tuned out and started to think about what I wanted to do. Actually I knew what I wanted to do, I just didn't know if I was smart enough. I had been reading on my own about the many worlds interpretation of quantum mechanics, and it was my current love. What it means is, whenever you make a choice between one event or the other, the universe splits in two. In one universe you've made one choice, and in the other you've made the other choice.

As an example, say Eddie asked me to the Homecoming Dance. He didn't, of course, since he assumed we were already going, but if he had, and, if I said yes, at that moment the universe would split in two. In one universe, I'd be going to the dance with Eddie. In the other, I wouldn't. In other words, you get to have your cake and eat it, too.

I heard my name and looked up. Mr. Rinaldi was smiling at me. "What about you Kathy? Any questions?"

"What about the many worlds interpretation of quantum mechanics?" I asked him.

"Where'd you hear about that?"

"I've been reading about it."

"Lots of luck," said Rinaldi, leading me to believe I was going over my head. I didn't care, though; I was enjoying going over my head.

After class I stopped by his desk. "Would it be possible for me to talk to you for a few minutes sometime?" I asked him.

"I've got a few minutes," he said.

"I have to get to my next class."

"When's your study hall?"

"Last period."

"I'm free then," he said. "Come to the office and we'll kick someone out of a cubicle and talk."

"Thanks."

"I just hope this isn't about the split-universe theory."

"No, it's something else."

"Good," he said, making me wonder if I better find another subject for my project.

* * *

My brother had the same lunch period as me, but usually I didn't see him. Probably because he usually wasn't in school. Today, though, he was not only there, he was surrounded by about a hundred kids, all wanting to know how it had been to be in a rock video. I could see him holding forth, looking every bit the young Hollywood director. Instead of dropping out of high school, he would probably end up in UCLA's film program.

"I'm jealous of Kevin," said Jennifer as soon as we sat down.

"You mean all the attention he's getting?"

"Next he'll probably get a part in a movie. I'm the one who wants to be an actress, and I'll be lucky if I get a part in the school play."

"I don't think he wants to be an actor," I told her. "I have a feeling he wants to direct. At least that's all he talked about at dinner last night."

"I'll bet your dad was thrilled to hear that. An artist and a director, just what he wanted."

"I think Dad will be thrilled if he just stays in school, at this point."

I heard someone say, "Hi, Kathy," and I looked up and saw Enid standing by the table. I also saw the stunned look on Jennifer's face.

"Hi, Enid," I said, "you want to sit with us?"

I felt Jennifer kick me under the table, but I ignored her. It wouldn't hurt to talk to someone else for a change.

Enid sat down next to me and I could see Jennifer looking her over.

"Nice blouse," said Jennifer, lying through her teeth.

"You really like it?" asked Enid.

"Looks sharp," said Jennifer.

"We were just talking about the Homecoming Dance," I said, and saw Jennifer give me a look as though I'd gone out of my mind.

"I'm going," said Enid.

"You're kidding!" said Jennifer, which wasn't very nice, but I couldn't blame her for being surprised, since I hadn't had a chance yet to tell her the news.

"That's great," I said, "who're you going with?" As if I didn't know.

"Gary Miller. He's in our class."

I nodded. Jennifer started to choke, but quickly recovered. "What're you wearing?" she asked Enid.

"I was hoping you'd tell me," she said to me. "I don't know what one wears to dances."

"It's Halloween," I said, "so you can wear a costume if you want."

"I'm wearing a slinky black dress," said Jennifer.

Enid looked a little pale at the thought of a slinky black dress.

"I'm just going in jeans," I said, to help her out. "I'll put on cowboy boots and a cowboy hat and it's my Western costume."

"The truth of it is, she refuses to wear heels," said Jennifer.

I nodded. "Yeah, that's the truth."

"I don't have anything to wear," said Enid, and I swear her voice sounded rusty from disuse.

Jennifer and I exchanged glances. "You want to go costume or regular?" she asked Enid.

I would've sworn she'd say costume, but she didn't.

"Well," I said. "The main thing is to be comfortable with whatever you choose."

"You could even wear a nice pair of pants," Jennifer said. Enid still looked kind of lost.

"We'll figure something out," I told Enid, wondering why she didn't ask her mom to buy her something.

And Enid, the girl I had been in awe of, the one I thought had mysterious powers, was smiling at us shyly like a little kid. There was hope for her yet.

My heart fluttered when I saw Mr. Rinaldi waiting for me outside the door to the office. When he saw me, he led the way inside and talked one of the counselors out of her office for a few minutes.

Acting very unlike a teacher, he took the chair in front of the desk and I got to sit behind it.

"So what's up, Kathy?" he said, sliding down in the chair and crossing his legs at the ankles. Except for his tie, he could've been one of the students. Come to think of it, even with his rocket ship tie he could've been one of the students.

"I sent in an application to Cal Tech."

He grinned at me in delight. "Great! Hey, I'm really happy to hear that."

"I don't think there's any chance they'll accept me, but—"

"Not accept you? You're exactly what they're looking for. And I'll write you a recommendation that'll knock their eyes out."

"Do you really think so? It seems like they're looking for students like Enid Cortelyou or Jason Green. I'm not a brain like that."

"Those guys got you bulldozed, Kathy?"

"I've been in classes with them. They know everything."

"Okay, Jason's pretty bright. Got a good mind. And I'm not saying Enid isn't bright. But I really like your creativity. You have a unique approach that could be invaluable as a physicist."

"If you're going by that quiz—"

"Sure I am. I couldn't believe some of the things you came up with."

"I was just using my imagination."

"I know."

All this approval from him was starting to get to me and I sat back and smiled.

"So?" he asked. "Any other problems?" If I hadn't had any, I would've thought some up.

"My dad wants me to go to UCLA."

"Good school, but not for you."

"He thinks it's more important to spend the money on my brothers' education." I was happy to see him roll his eyes.

"So put in for a scholarship."

"You think I'd get one? It's not like I'm some science whiz or a minority student or anything."

"I can't swear you'll get a full one, but I bet you could get a partial. Anyway, it's worth a try. I'll get hold of an application for you."

"You're going to an awful lot of trouble for me," I said, suddenly getting a little nervous about the fact that he really did seem to like me. What if he said something like, *Maybe we could see each other sometime.* What would I do then?

"Hey, I'd just like you for a classmate," he said, and my stomach began to do tap dances.

"What do you mean?"

"I mean I'm going to Cal Tech for my doctorate."

Was he trying to tell me it would be all right for us to date then? Oh, my God. I saw us walking to class together on the Cal Tech campus—kissing good-bye at the classroom door—maybe living together. . . .

"You're going back to school?" I asked, my voice sounding a little strained.

"Yeah. I don't mind teaching high school, but my heart is really in research."

"You're a good teacher."

"Yes, but I want to be a physicist. Just like you."

He was smiling at me, his eyes holding mine, and now I was really getting nervous.

"When are you going?" I asked.

"I figure I'll be able to manage it financially in two more years," he said. I would be a sophomore by then.

"Well, that's great," I said, trying to think of a way to end the conference in a hurry. I was getting so nervous.

He did it for me. "Much as I enjoy talking to you, Kathy, I've got to go see the principal about taking a day off next week."

"I really want to thank you," I said.

"My pleasure."

"I mean it. Your class has changed my life," I blurted out, then felt incredibly stupid.

"That's good to hear. Because I really wasn't crazy about the idea of teaching school at first.

Someday, though, I may be able to point to you and say, 'If it weren't for me . . .' "

He had more confidence in me than I had, but if he believed in me, well, maybe I could make it. And if I didn't, it sure wasn't going to be from lack of trying.

Jennifer walked into my room, put her hands around her throat and made a strangling noise.

"It's Albert Einstein, for your information," I told her, shoving her into the room and closing the door.

"I know who it is," she said. "I'm not a complete moron, you know. It's just more what I'd expect to find in Enid's bedroom. Too bad you can't get a poster of that good-looking teacher of yours."

"Do you think he could really be interested in me, Jen?" I said suddenly.

"Ah ha! so you admit you're interested," she said.

"Don't ask *me*. What do you think?"

"Well, he was talking about . . ." I broke off, suddenly remembering that I hadn't told her about Cal Tech yet.

"He was talking about what?" she asked, not missing a thing.

"Well, he's going to—"

"He's going to what? Spill it, Kathy."

"You're going to be mad at me."

"I'm going to be madder if you don't tell me."

"He's going to write me a letter of recommendation for Cal Tech."

Not a muscle moved in Jennifer's face.

"That doesn't mean I'll be accepted."

Nothing.

"Oh, Jen, I really want to go there. It's not like it's that far from UCLA. We could still see each other all the time."

"I'm thinking of going to New York."

"What?"

"Robert says actors don't need to go to college. He says the best thing to do is go to New York and take acting lessons."

"Your mother is going to let you go to New York."

"Is your father letting you go to Cal Tech?"

"No. But I'm going to go anyway, if they let me in."

"Right."

"Just when were you going to tell me about this?"

"As soon as you told me."

"You *knew*?"

"I had a pretty good idea. So what's this got to do with Rinaldi maybe being interested in you?"

"He said he was going there, too. For his doctorate. I don't know; it just sounded a little personal the way he was talking."

"Well, Kath, if you're both in college, then there's nothing wrong with it. You'll both be adults, right?"

"I'll bet he's experienced."

"So what? Eddie would be experienced if you gave him half a chance. And speaking of which, does Eddie know about this yet? I have a feeling he's not going to take it quite as well as I am."

That was something I didn't even want to think about. Because if it came down to a choice between Eddie and Cal Tech, the universe better split in two, because that would be the only solution.

15

THE NIGHT OF THE DANCE CAME AND WE WERE READY, me in my cowboy gear and Jennifer in her slinky black dress and a tall, pointy witch's hat. Eddie and Alan were going to pick us up. Alan, not Steve, because Jennifer decided not to go back with Steve. She thought being involved with someone seriously would interfere with her career. She was giving up love in the interests of stardom.

The boys came and made the appropriate wolf whistles when they saw us. Eddie really did look handsome. He was wearing a plaid shirt and farmer's overalls, and he had a blade of grass stuck in his teeth.

"Howdy, ma'am," he said, handing me my corsage. I got ready to ooh and aah, then looked in the clear cellophane box and laughed.

"Where did you get this?"

Eddie grinned.

"You like it? I thought it was you."

I opened the box and picked up my corsage.

Nestled among the white baby's breath were three perfect, golden, stalks of—wheat.

"What'd you do? Fly this in from Kansas?"

"Nothing's too good for my baby." Eddie pinned the corsage carefully to my chambray shirt. Then he smiled, stood back, and kissed his fingertips.

"Perfect!"

I laughed and put my arms around his neck, pulling his head down for a kiss. As I hugged him, I felt suddenly very close to him again. Who else would put up with my changeable moods? Who else would have come with me to look for Kevin without a question? And, who else would give his girlfriend a wheat-stalk corsage? Eddie Lenahan was pretty great.

We got to the dance and immediately split up into the boys' group and the girls' group, as tradition demanded.

Jennifer and I got some punch—it was early and no one had spiked it yet. Suddenly Jennifer grabbed my arm.

"Look!" she hissed. "Over there. Enid!"

I took a quick gulp of punch and looked to where Jennifer was pointing. Sure enough, Enid and Gary Miller were standing uncertainly by the door. Enid was looking around the room and when her gaze fell on me, I smiled and waved. She smiled back tentatively. Then Gary saw Bobby Garner (who had come with Susie) and Gary and Enid crossed the threshold into teenage normalcy: Gary went to stand by Bobby, and Enid came over to me and Jennifer.

I have to admit, Gary and Enid did not make that bad of a couple. True, Gary looked like he was wearing his little brother's suit with the hems let down. But he didn't look so awful. I could see how for Enid he might be—if not Prince Charming—then certainly an acceptable date for her first dance.

And Enid herself had made big strides in the past few weeks. She still didn't wear enough eye makeup—maybe she never would. But she looked okay. She looked very—Enid.

She was wearing her black leotard and a big, full, swirly, purple Indian-print skirt. Over her leotard she had an embroidered vest. She looked downright festive.

She smiled when she saw my corsage.

"That Eddie," I said, noticing her glance. "He knows me all too well."

"So how's Gary?" Jennifer asked in her usual, subtle fashion.

"He's—he's fine," Enid said. "We really don't know each other that well. I think he was kind of surprised when I asked him to the dance."

Jennifer choked on her punch and I slapped her on the back—hard.

"Well, don't worry," I said encouragingly. "Every couple has to start somewhere."

"It must be nice to be with someone who knows you well," Enid said, gesturing at my corsage.

Her observation surprised me.

"Yeah, I guess it is," I agreed. "It's comfortable. Easy." Tonight, that's how it seemed. A few weeks ago it had seemed predictable and boring.

But ever since I had discovered physics, so many things in my life had turned unpredictable: my brother Mike dropping out of premed, my brother Kevin *not* dropping out of school, Jennifer and her non-reunion with Steve, Jennifer moving to New York, me not only deciding on my college major, but on the rest of my life . . . Suddenly having Eddie as the only constant in my life seemed very reassuring. Rinaldi was adorable but I was coming back down to earth.

I looked for Eddie across the room, but my view was blocked by someone standing in front of me.

He was dressed all in black with a black mask over his eyes, but I knew it was Mr. Rinaldi by the way he moved and his curly hair.

"Want to dance?" he asked me. It wasn't unheard of for the chaperons to dance with the students, and anyway, I was glad he had asked. I figured I was through fantasizing about him, but it would be nice to have this one dance. And if I was lucky, Eddie—over talking football with the rest of the team—wouldn't even notice.

I looked at Jennifer and Enid. Jennifer raised her brows and nodded. I moved into his arms. It was a slow song, something from the sixties that sounded vaguely familiar. I was thinking, *I'm actually dancing with him. This is like one of my fantasies.* And it was okay because there were lots of people around. And because I had just fallen in love—with my boyfriend.

"Do you mind having to chaperon, Mr. Rinaldi?"

I asked him. What kind of conversation do you have with a teacher you're dancing with?

"When we're at Cal Tech you can call me Tom," he said, smiling down at me. He was tall, but not quite as tall as Eddie. After being next to Eddie's solid football player body for two years, it was interesting to hold someone who was skinnier.

I smiled back noncommittally. I blushed when I remembered my fantasies about living with Mr. Rinaldi, or kissing him, or . . .

"You okay, Kathy?"

"Oh, yeah, um hmmm . . ." Just having a major embarrassment attack.

"So what's going to happen to you and Lenahan when you graduate?" Rinaldi asked.

My cheeks burned again. I had an idea that this was a slightly-less-than-teacherish question.

"I don't know," I answered truthfully. "I think he wants to stay together, but I don't know how he's going to feel about me going to Cal Tech."

Rinaldi nodded. His hand, holding mine, was dry and warm.

"You don't have to marry your first serious boyfriend, you know," Rinaldi said pleasantly, looking over my shoulder at the other couples.

My eyes widened. I didn't know where to look. What was he saying? What did this mean? I licked my lips and stared blindly over his shoulder. My eyes fell on Eddie, watching me from across the room. He smiled gently and raised his glass to me. I smiled back.

Suddenly I relaxed. All Rinaldi had said was that

I didn't have to marry my first serious boyfriend. True enough.

I pulled back and smiled at Rinaldi.

"Maybe we'll have a class together," I said as the song ended and couples broke apart.

"Maybe so. Thanks for the dance, Kathy." He began to move away, then turned to call after me, "Oh, by the way, there's a major test next week." His smile widened as he disappeared into the throng of dancers leaving the floor.

I stood rooted to the spot, then threw back my head and laughed.

It was the last dance, a slow one, and I was resting in Eddie's arms. His arms were as familiar to me as my own bed, and just as comforting.

"I've got to talk to you," I said.

"You asking for permission?"

"Seriously. We have to have a serious talk."

I felt him tense up a little, as though he was afraid I was going to break up with him. I guess I hadn't been so great lately, so I moved in a little closer to reassure him.

His arms tightened around me. "Can you give me a hint?"

"It's about us."

He stopped dancing and looked down at me. "What's the matter?"

"I want to talk, that's all. There's something I have to tell you."

"I'm not sure I want to hear this," he said, his face growing serious.

"I'm not sure you do, either." I said shakily.

All my plans relied on him being supportive.

"Kath," he said, his eyes looking stricken, and then he swallowed whatever else he was going to say.

"Can we go somewhere alone where we can talk?"

"You don't want to go out with the others?"

I shook my head.

"Sure, let's go," he said, taking my hand and leading me off the dance floor. He was walking a little stiffly and I didn't think it was from the football game.

I was sure now that he thought I was going to break up with him. I didn't want to cause him that kind of anxiety, so I said, "I love you, Eddie."

He didn't look relieved. "What was that for, to soften the blow?"

"It's not something like that," I said, although it was something like that. It was something that was going to change our lives, another of those universe-splitting decisions.

"Want to get something to eat?" he asked me.

"Could we just drive down to the beach? We can get something to eat afterward." Although afterward he might prefer to take me straight home.

He didn't drive to Huntington Beach, though, but kept driving down the highway in the direction of Newport Beach. I guessed he was in no hurry to hear what I was going to say.

He had passed Newport and was still headed south, driving fast, not saying a word, when I said, "Eddie, if you keep going, we'll end up in Mexico."

"Want to elope to Mexico?" he asked, sounding pretty upset.

I took off my cowboy hat and threw it in the backseat, then moved over closer to him, and leaned my head on his shoulder. "Eddie, what I want to talk to you about has nothing to do with you."

"Nothing?"

"I'm not breaking up with you, if that's what you're thinking."

"Well, in that case," said Eddie, pulling off the highway and heading down a dark road, "let's get it over with."

I had thought maybe we could walk on the beach, but the car would do just as well.

He made a right and ended up in a cul-de-sac, parking under a streetlight at the very end in front of a house with the light from a television set in the window. He turned off the engine and put his arm around me. "Well, let's hear it."

I moved away from him and leaned against the door. I wanted to be able to see his face while we talked.

"I applied to Cal Tech," I said, getting straight to the point.

Eddie looked a little mystified. "And?"

"That's it," I said. "I'd really like to go there."

"It's physics, isn't it?"

I nodded.

"When did you decide this?"

"After the field trip. It was just a whim at first, but then I was talking to Rinaldi and he thinks I have a chance of getting in."

"Rinaldi, huh?"

"He's been very helpful."

"What's this with you and this Rinaldi?"

"Nothing, Eddie. It's physics I'm interested in, not Rinaldi."

"I saw you dancing with him."

"I saw you dancing with a sexy sophomore, but you don't hear me complaining about it, do you?"

"You told your folks about Cal Tech?" he asked.

"Dad says he can't afford it. He thinks I should be a dental technician so that I can help you out."

"Yeah, I can really see you as my office assistant."

"Rinaldi thinks I might be able to get some kind of scholarship. And I'm going to save all the money I make."

Eddie was looking straight out the windshield now, nodding his head. "So you want to be a physicist, is that it?"

"Yes."

"What a relief!"

"I knew you thought I was going to break up with you."

He turned and grinned at me. "No, I mean, *what a relief!* If you're going to be a physicist, I won't have to be a dentist."

"I thought you wanted to be a dentist."

"What, are you kidding me? *Want* to be a dentist? Who in his right mind wants to drill people's teeth all day?"

"Really? Do you mean that?"

"Hey, listen, it's a good living, I'm not knocking it. It seemed like a good way to support you and the kids. But if you're going to be a physicist, you can support us."

"I can't believe you want to be a housewife, Eddie."

"No, I want to be a football coach. So what does that mean, being a physicist? A couple of degrees?"

"A doctorate, I guess."

"We can do it," he said, sounding as happy and excited as a little kid. "By the time you get to grad school, I should be working and you won't even have to ask your father for any money."

"It's not that far from UCLA."

"I know where Cal Tech is. We can get an apartment halfway between them. We've both got cars, it'll be no problem."

"What's your dad going to say if you don't go to dental school?"

"What can he say? He loves football as much as I do."

"Oh, Eddie, I can't wait," I said, throwing myself in his arms.

"You mean this is finally the night?" he said, but I could tell he was teasing.

"That's not what I meant. Anyway, I'm starving."

But who knows, maybe it would be the night. Whether we did or didn't do it, and when, suddenly didn't seem that important anymore.

Eddie turned to me. "Want to live it up and go down to the Carousel?" he asked, mentioning an expensive restaurant in Laguna Beach.

"No, let's just go to Fatso's," I said.

"Good idea," said Eddie. "We've got to start saving our money."

I reached over and kissed Eddie as he started up the car. "Did I tell you about the split-universe theory?" I asked him.

He groaned. "You starting that again?"

"You better get used to it."

"Well, as soon as you're finished, I'm going to tell you about this new play the coach came up with."

I couldn't wait.

About the Author

BEVERLY SOMMERS is the author of young adult novels as well as adult romances.